ESPECIALLY FOR GIRLS™ presents

Belonging

•

by Virginia M. Scott

KENDALL GREEN PUBLICATIONS
Gallaudet College Press   Washington, D.C.

Published 1986 by Gallaudet College Press,
Washington, DC 20002
© 1986 by Virginia M. Tibbs. All rights reserved
Printed in the United States of America

Scott, Virginia M., 1945–
  Belonging.
  Summary: After contracting meningitis, a fifteen-year-old girl becomes deaf and
must struggle with accepting her hearing loss and being accepted by her friends and
family.
  [1. Deaf—Fiction. 2. Physically handicapped—
Fiction] I. Title.
PZ7.S4294Be   1986   [Fic]   85-31135
ISBN 0-930323-14-9

The Good Listener

·

For a long time last fall the only one I felt close to was my cat. Jasmine, a Siamese with eyes the color of a summer sky, would just stare at me, and most of the time the sleepy cat's eyelids drifted shut while I talked to her.

Talking to a cat has its limits.

"You're getting antisocial, Gustie Blaine," I frequently told myself.

It hadn't always been this way. I mean, I was never as bubbly as Sara Marler, who attracted friends like a magnet. Sara used to be my best friend. She is blonde, the captain of the cheerleaders, and her curves curve where they are supposed to. I'm less blonde, I used to be a cheerleader, and my curves almost don't. Still, I had a lot of friends and wasn't exactly Little Miss Hopeless. Or at least I never used to be.

I met Sara about eleven years ago. The Marlers bought a house a block down the street from ours then, and Sara and I became instant friends. I'm not sure why. Even at five, Sara and I were very different from each other. Oh, we liked to do the same things, like playing "store" or Barbies, but Sara was a born leader and I was more a follower. I was usually the student to her teacher, the patient to her doctor, and the willing accomplice to her sometimes stupid ideas.

I'll give you some examples. About three years ago, I liked Jerry

Buckner. He lived across the street from us, but I never noticed how cute he was until I was twelve and Jerry was thirteen. No doubt my good old sandbox buddy from toddler days still saw me as the little girl he'd always known. I wanted to let him know I had grown up and I liked him. How to do it was the problem.

It was Sara who came up with a foolproof way to get Jerry's attention.

"Jerry will rescue you!" she told me.

"Rescue me? What from?" I asked, pretending to be afraid. "Are you going to tie me to the railroad tracks?"

"No, silly."

"Then what?"

Sara thought for a little while and then got that light bulb look she gets when an idea hits. She was glowing. This idea was going to be a doozy.

"You're going to climb that old apple tree in your backyard and get stuck. Jerry will help you down."

Personally, I thought it was a dumb idea, but what could I tell Sara? I didn't want to spoil her fun. Then, too, maybe it would work. Almost anything was worth one of Jerry Buckner's smiles, even though he wore braces and I hated climbing trees.

That's how I ended up in the apple tree. After Sara's coaxing, I found myself high into the tree's sturdy limbs. At that height, I really doubted that I could get down on my own.

According to the plan, Sara ran across the street to get Jerry. We knew he was home because his bike was in the Buckners' yard.

Every once in a while, I let out a "Help! Help!" Fortunately, my parents were out shopping.

I thought Sara would never get back. I felt like I'd been up there forever when she finally came racing around the corner of the house. But it wasn't Jerry she had with her. Just as I let out a really worried "Help," I saw Jerry's *father* coming toward me.

So much for Sara's foolproof idea.

Earlier, when we were only nine or ten, we were into ghosts and vampires and things like that. There was this huge brick mansion on the way to school. The For Sale sign had been in the yard so long, it was getting rusty. Mom called the old Henderson house a white elephant. Lots of kids said it was haunted.

One day when Sara and I were walking home from school, she started telling me a story.

I remember the day because it was when I accidentally spilled Prell all over Jerry Buckner's head. This was before I liked him. Anyway, Sara and I had gone to the store on the way home from school. When Jerry and some other guys started pestering us, Sara told me to bop Jerry on the head. It was only a plastic bottle, and Jerry really was being a pest. I wasn't going to clobber him, of course, but I pretended I was. Well, we couldn't believe it when the cap came loose and the soap went all over Jerry's head. He looked like a miniature Green Giant.

After the guys left us, Sara started telling me a story about the old Henderson place.

"Have you ever wondered about the old man who lived here?" she asked. We were standing in front of the brick house by then.

"My mom told me that no one knows much about him."

"That's for sure, and you wouldn't believe why."

"Why?"

"Why wouldn't you believe?"

Maybe it was Sara's conscience that made her ask that. I could tell she was probably making this up, but I always enjoyed her imaginative stories and usually played along.

I said, "No. I meant, why doesn't anyone know much about Mr. Henderson?"

The weather seemed to cooperate with the mysterious mood Sara was trying to create. Right before she answered, a gust of wind blew through the piles of October leaves. I felt a sudden chill, just like people are supposed to feel in spooky books and movies.

Sara leaned close to me, looked both ways, and whispered, "He was a jewel thief."

"Sure," I thought.

Each day that week, Sara added a little more to the story as we passed the house. Each day I listened and acted as if I fell for the tale, but I could tell that Sara's storytelling juices were working overtime.

At Sara's urging, we carefully watched the window shades of the house. Since no one lived there, I didn't expect to see any change in them.

"Look," Sara ordered one day as we walked past the house.

"At what?"

"The second floor, second window from the left. The shade isn't even with the rest of the shades on that floor."

"So?"

"So! Gustie, it was even before! Something moved it!"

I could almost see Sara's exclamation points in the air.

"Some *thing*?" I asked, trying to act scared. Sara probably wanted me to believe, or pretend to believe, that the ghostly fingers of the late Mr. Henderson had moved the shade.

Expecting her to try to convince me otherwise, I said, "You know I don't believe in ghosts."

"I'm not so sure about that, old friend. Anyhow, I didn't mean a ghost. Don't you get it?"

"Nope."

"One of Mr. Henderson's accomplices is hiding out in the house!"

Sara succeeded in getting a startled reaction from me. Had that shade been even with the other shades yesterday? Could Sara's wild tale of international jewel theft be true? Was there even a treasure hidden somewhere inside the house?

But no, a few days later Sara confessed that her story was made up and that she didn't know a thing about Mr. Henderson.

"Oh you," I told her with affection.

Then she said something I'll never forget.

"Gustie, do you know why you're the perfect friend for me?"

"No, why?"

"Very simple, You're a good listener, whether it's something silly like the haunted house or something more serious like when Grandpa died."

Well, times sure changed. Last fall, I spent a lot of time alone in my bedroom. Whenever I thought about the past, I felt a lump in my throat. Sara and I shared so many memories. Maybe memories aren't enough, though.

Sara didn't come over anymore. She hadn't changed. But I, you see, was different. I, the good listener, was deaf now.

The End of Summer Fun

•

My problems all started last July. I could still hear then. It was a really hot month, so Sara and I and two other girls spent lots of time getting tan and having a blast at Pine Lake. We'd lie side by side on our towels and talk mostly about how we looked and, of course, guys.

"Do you think I'd look better with a nose job?" Cindy Kreighton asked, fingering a nose that was kind of upturned and on the short side. The zillion freckles scattered over her face somehow went with the nose.

"I like your nose," I told her.

"Yeah, me, too," Sara seconded. "It's . . ."

"Don't say it," Cindy broke in.

"Say what?" Dana Arlington asked.

"C-u-t-e," Sara said, spelling out the word.

Cindy groaned and said, "That's why I don't like it. Who wants to be just . . . cute?" She wrinkled her nose as she said the last word.

"I don't think they do nose jobs to make noses longer anyway," Dana said. "Just shorter. Besides, think of yourself as being . . . hmm . . ."

When a word didn't come to her, I put it in, "Elfin."

"Yeah," Dana said, taking in more than just Cindy's face. Cindy had to stand tall just to reach the even five feet she claimed to be.

"Like a pixie," Sara offered.

"Yeah?" Cindy asked in a voice that sounded more hopeful.

"Yeah," we all chorused, nodding our heads to convince Cindy.

Suddenly feeling uncomfortable in the heat, I started to get up, saying, "I'm roasting."

"Wait," Cindy said, nose problem seemingly forgotten. "Did you see that hunk that just walked by?"

"Which one?" Sara asked. We all laughed.

"He's walking toward the parking lot. In the cut-offs and light blue shirt."

Three pairs of eyes, including mine, searched and locked on the unsuspecting guy Cindy had singled out.

"Let's go!" Dana joked. "He's at least a 9."

But they were hot, too, so we headed toward the cool water of the lake instead.

Even more than I remember our usual conversations, whenever I think back to the days at the beach, I remember sensations. Sensations like

> . . . the hot, prickly feel of the sun just before I gave in and dashed down to the water;
>
> . . . the scent of Coppertone and grilled hot dogs;
>
> . . . the sight of browning bodies, bikinis of all colors, and skiers showing off on the lake that makes our small Midwestern town the kind of place where people want to live; and
>
> . . . the jumble of sounds—whooping yells and sudden splashes, snatches of conversations, laughter, a jet flying high overhead, and radios.

It's funny about the radios. It was a radio that made me notice Jack Reilly.

I was in that state of half-sleep you can be in when the sun is making you feel dopey and carefree. I had been thinking about Mom's birthday and the charm I was going to give her to go on her gold chain. It was the tiniest seashell, and I knew Mom would love it. Her favorite place was the ocean. Before she came to the Midwest, Mom lived in

7

Oregon, in a little town right on the coast. Every time we went there to visit my grandparents, Mom spent lots of time beachcombing.

"I like everything about the sea," she would tell me, "even its treachery. Life itself is like that, with polarities of good and bad, beautiful and forbidding. Perhaps the sea is all the more awesome because it's always changing its moods. It's so beautiful that it almost hurts."

Polarities was one of Mom's favorite words; it means opposites, like white and black, or happy and sad.

I was just beginning to think of Gram and Gramps when I heard the radio. It wasn't a station I usually heard at the beach. At that moment, *Rhapsody in Blue* was playing.

Maybe I'm some kind of weirdo, but classical music (and symphonic jazz, like *Rhapsody in Blue*) is my favorite. I can't explain what it does to me. Sometimes I want to cry because the feeling is so beautiful it almost hurts. It's a little like Mom and the sea.

I could hardly hear the station. It wasn't as if it was blasting. I listened to it a while before raising myself onto my elbows to look for the radio's owner. It took a minute, but I traced the music to a yellow beach towel. Lying on it was a guy with black hair and a great body. He was lying on his stomach, wearing black-and-white checked trunks.

I didn't realize that I was staring at him until *Rhapsody in Blue* was almost over. Actually, I hadn't been staring at him. After I checked him out as the radio's owner, I was looking in his direction and not really seeing him, if you know what I mean. My mind was soaking up the music more than it was taking in the guy.

As the music stopped, I came out of my trance and found him staring back at me. I knew it wasn't because of our radio because it was silent at the moment. And he wasn't looking at Sara, Dana, or Cindy, because they were all at the food stand getting Cokes.

We smiled at each other, and I felt a tingle inside me when he walked toward my towel. I wished I had on my striped bikini instead of the boring old one-piece.

"Was my radio bothering you?" he asked.

"No," I told him, noticing that his eyes were an unexpectedly brilliant blue that almost matched my cat Jasmine's. You would think that anyone with such black hair and bronzed skin would have different eyes. "*Rhapsody in Blue* is a favorite of mine. It's just that usually I hear Top 40 stations at the beach."

He smiled. "You like classical music?"

"It's my favorite," I admitted.

We talked about music. I told him I'd taken piano lessons for six years. He told me he had for ten years. Then we realized that we didn't even know each other's names.

"I'm Jack Reilly," he said.

"Gustie Blaine," I offered.

"Gustie? That's an unusual name." I thought he'd add a joke about it, asking as so many people did if I was born on a windy day. But Jack didn't.

"It's short for Augusta," I explained. "It's a family name."

"I like it."

And I like him!

As it happened, though, there wasn't time for me to see Jack Reilly on the beach again before the curtain fell on my summer.

Just A Little Headache

•

Nobody knows for sure just where I picked up the terrible disease called meningitis, but it could have been at the beach or maybe at Jacob's where Sara and I often stopped for a burger and fries.

The illness started with just a little headache. I didn't say anything to Mom at first. I just took two aspirins. I thought it would go away like most headaches do. Anyway, Mom and I had planned to spend the day shopping, and I didn't want to spoil the plans.

Mom and I were looking forward to shopping for a present for my cousin Bonnie's new baby. Bonnie and little Emily were just home from the hospital, and, of course, Mom and I could hardly wait to see the new baby. I love little kids; I hoped I would get to baby-sit my newest cousin.

Mom looked very pretty that day. It was hot, but she looked cool in her wraparound skirt and lime green T-shirt. The green made Mom's reddish hair look very bright. She usually wore her hair down around her shoulders, but that day she had put it up to keep her neck cool. Her new gold seashell glistened on its chain. Looking over her figure, I hoped mine would turn out as well. I had my doubts.

"I wonder if the baby looks like Bonnie," Mom remarked as we looked over tiny dresses in sherbet colors. "I should have asked Brad about her hair, but he was so excited on the phone that I forgot."

Hair color could be an important factor in choosing a dress because

Bonnie had the brightest, reddest hair you've ever seen. Mom's was more of a copper color, but Bonnie's was really orange-red. It clashed with lots of colors. Mom and I wondered if the baby had gotten Bonnie's hair.

"How about the blue one or the mint green?" I suggested. Most of the dresses were in pink. Personally, my favorite was a blue one with little puffed sleeves and a smocked top.

"I like . . . this one." The pause was very long, or at least it seemed to be. A pain in my head made time stop and I forgot everything else.

I don't remember Mom paying for the dress or leaving the shop. We were out on the sidewalk in front of the store when Mom saw Helen Burke, the mayor's wife, and stopped to talk. I don't know what they said. I can remember standing there and smiling now and then. I can remember feeling very hot in the sun. But most of all, I remember the pain. It was like a big hand was squeezing the base of my head, which felt stiff and sore. The pain seemed to fly up from my neck and into my whole head, where it bounced around in echoes. I wanted to put my arms over my head and try to block it out.

I realized that Mom and Mrs. Burke had stopped talking. I said good-bye to Mrs. Burke, and then Mom and I walked to the car. She put the wrapped baby gift on the back seat. We were going to drop it off at Bonnie's on the way home.

A big wave of pain hit me while Mom was starting the car. This time, I couldn't resist putting my hands up to my head, and Mom saw me do it.

"Is anything wrong? Head hurt?"

In the understatement of my life, I told her, "A little."

"Maybe we should go home. You can take a couple of aspirins, rest a little, and we can go see the baby later. How does that sound?"

Mom didn't know I'd already taken two pills. Yet as awful as I felt, I thought it was just from the heat. I still wanted to go see the baby. I was even willing to wait in the car while Mom did, especially if she thought the baby might catch something from me. I supposed I could be coming down with the flu, even though it felt different. I even thought that by going to Bonnie's, I could wish away the pain.

"I'll be fine, Mom. It's just a little headache from the heat."

But Mom had driven only a half a mile when the pain got even worse.

"Oh, my head," I moaned as I lowered it into my lap. My neck felt even stiffer than before, and my entire head felt as if it were being crushed. "Mom, my head. It hurts so much." When I realized that I was talking into my lap, I turned toward Mom. The pain was making me cry.

"Let's go home and get you fixed up," she said.

I loved her very much right then. I knew she was disappointed she would have to postpone the trip to Bonnie's, but it was obvious that her concern for me was a lot more important.

I don't remember much that happened after we got home. Just the pain. I suppose Mom gave me those aspirins she had mentioned, but they did not help. I suppose she put a cool, wet cloth on my forehead, but it did not make the pain go away either. Maybe I screamed out loud with the pain. Or maybe it was just my body screaming inside.

The last thing I remember is the ambulance coming to take me to the hospital. I remember smiling at the guys with the stretcher as they wheeled me down the hallway in our house. I looked up at one of the men and said, "I'm not that sick."

But I was.

I don't remember the ambulance ride to the hospital, and I don't remember the Emergency Room doctors. In fact, I don't remember anything at all—no dreams even—until I woke in a hospital bed two days later. A doctor was cutting a little hole in my ankle for a feeding tube. I know it sounds yucky, but I didn't feel any pain. I went back to sleep.

When I woke up, Mom was there. She was wearing an aqua summer dress; Dad was beside her. I could see the love in their eyes and their happy expressions when I opened my eyes. I don't remember if we said anything. I guess I was too sick. But I remember the feeling of love, and I think I smiled back at them.

For the next few days I was in and out of sleep a lot, just sort of drifting. My head didn't ache anymore, but I didn't have any energy. I could hardly move. I didn't ask what was wrong with me, and nobody told me that I had meningitis. I knew I was very sick, though.

I also knew that something weird was going on with my hearing. It was sort of like people were talking to me from the next room, like there was a wall between them and me that kept me from hearing even the closest ones clearly. I thought it was just from the drugs the doctors were giving me to keep me alive.

I remember odd things about being in the hospital. One of my favorite things was when a nurse came in each night and rubbed my back with Dermassage. I'll never forget that smell.

And I remember getting a get well card that made me smile. It wasn't that funny, but it made me feel good at the time. The front was a picture of a bright red apple with the caption, "An apple a day keeps the doctor away . . ." The inside had a picture of a goofy-looking giant holding a whole uprooted apple tree and saying, ". . . so look what I brung you."

I got lots of cards and flowers and even some gifts and candy. The nurses finally let me put on a new nightgown, but I couldn't eat any candy or use the paint-by-number sets. Even reading made me tired. At the end of the first week in the hospital, I still had trouble sitting up in bed.

It was pretty quiet in the hospital. I wasn't allowed to have visitors because meningitis is very contagious and because I was so weak. Dad, who is an obstetrician came in to see me every morning when he made hospital rounds (that's when doctors go to the hospital to see how their patients are doing). Even Dad hadn't known that I had meningitis until I got to the hospital, went into a coma, and had some tests. The doctors took fluid out of my spinal column, for one thing, and it wasn't clear like spinal fluid is supposed to be.

Mom also came to visit every day, only in the afternoons. She used to be a nurse, so helping me eat or use the bedpan came naturally for her. She was very gentle but also very sure of how to do things.

Some of Dad's doctor friends stopped in to say hi when they were on their rounds. Dr. Kreisler, who is very short and has real bushy hair, stopped in each morning. He wore a different hat every day. My favorite was a Mickey Mouse hat with giant black ears. Everybody at the hospital loves Dr. Kreisler.

During my second week in the hospital, I continued to sleep most of the time. When I was awake, I didn't do much because I felt so weak and tired. I liked to look out the large window to the left of my bed. There were lots of brightly colored zinnias blooming in a narrow flower bed near my window. Every day, I watched the gardener pick off the wilted blossoms and water the plants. When I got stronger, I realized that the gardener came at 11:30 each morning, like clockwork. As I said, you notice strange things in a hospital.

Little by little, I got better and my routine changed. I went from being fed through IV needles, to a liquid diet, and on to soft foods like custard. I stayed awake for longer stretches, and I got better at sitting up and doing simple things like reading or brushing my hair. Finally, after I'd been in the hospital for about ten days, the doctors decided I could go home. Don't get me wrong; I wasn't that strong—I had to go home by ambulance. I wouldn't have gone at all if I hadn't had a doctor and a nurse in the family.

My room at home never looked better to me. It is a color I always think of as candied violet. It's a really pretty medium purple. One of my aunts used to bring us some little candy violets just that color every time she came to visit us from Oregon. The carpet in my room is a shade or two lighter than the walls, and the bedspread and drapes have bouquets of lilacs against a cream-colored background. Not everything matched, though. I had several posters on the walls, and Emma, my stuffed toy flamingo from our trip to Florida, was a coral color that didn't look so hot with the candied violet. The bookshelf that Sara and I had put up on our own was a little crooked. But the room looked great to me, especially when Jasmine hopped into my bed and happily kneaded me with her paws as she purred up a storm.

My first meal at home was weird, but it was what I was hungry for. I had bean with bacon soup and a kind of cellophane-wrapped jelly roll that normally I don't like.

My lilac-patterened sheets were a welcome change from hospital white. The sheets, plus a zillion other little details, made my first couple of days back at home seem wonderful. But after a few days, I started getting frustrated. I mean, there I was at home, with everything looking just as it had before I'd gotten sick, yet, *I* felt so different. Each familiar object I saw only reminded me how unfamiliar I felt inside, like the real me was gone and an invalid was taking my place.

All the time I was in the hospital, I looked forward to going home. In the way of daydreams, going home had meant going back to the way I'd been before the trip to the hospital. Oh sure, I knew I'd have to stay in bed for a while, but I really believed that most of my physical problems would melt away very quickly once I was on my own turf.

They didn't, though, and I felt more and more impatient. I couldn't even get up to go to the bathroom on my own. My legs weren't paralyzed or anything, but I was still weak from meningitis. I could walk a little, but I needed to lean on someone.

Mom had given me a little bell to ring when I needed her for bathroom help or something else. Although at first I thought the bell was sort of neat—it reminded me of the way people in old movies and books used bells to summon their servants—it got so that each time I rang it, I felt like throwing it at my closet door. I felt so helpless. I couldn't do anything. I was dependent on someone else for everything, even something as simple as making it down a short hall to the bathroom. I hated it.

I continued to sleep a lot. I also read a lot of historical fiction, especially about the era of Mary, Queen of Scots. Sometimes, I played "mouse" with Jasmine. I'd throw a toy mouse and she'd retrieve it like a dog does a stick.

Whenever I woke up in the morning or from a nap, I had the renewed hope that my hearing had gone back to normal. I felt a fresh letdown whenever Mom or Dad came into my room, said something, and I realized nothing had changed. I always felt like I had a set of earplugs in my ears. I tried swallowing hard, thinking I could pop my ears open as you do in an elevator or on a plane. Each time I tried something like that and it didn't work, I panicked.

Was this going to last? Shouldn't my hearing be back to normal by now? Would I go through my life saying "What?" when a sentence sounded something like, *Mumble mumble feel better mumble mumble?* While I was in the hospital, I was too busy just fighting for my life to even think much about my weird hearing, but I knew now I was out of danger and would live. Wasn't it time for me to shrug this off like I had the chicken pox or the flu?

About the time all this was going through my mind, I became aware that I wasn't hearing anything out of my right ear. Looking back, it had probably been that way from the time I came out of the coma in the hospital. I didn't notice it, though, until Mom shampooed my hair—I could hear the water rushing over my left ear but not my right one. Later, as my hair was drying naturally, I tried an experiment.

Snap. A finger snap beside my left ear had a familiar crispness to it.

Snap. When I did the same thing next to my right ear, the sound was muffled. It carried around to my left ear almost as if a door was shut on the right side and the sound sought entrance by traveling to the open door on the other side of my head.

I also began to notice that I could hear people better if they were either in front of me or to my left. There were lots of mumbles and blanks in conversation if whoever was talking spoke on my right side.

I probably asked my parents three or four times every day when my hearing would get better, but they just told me to give it time.

As I felt stronger physically, I got to do more things. One day Mom walked into my bedroom with Dad right behind her carrying their bedroom TV set. I got pretty excited; the TV would be a nice break from reading, napping, and mouse tossing.

Dad said something, but his voice was muffled. Only the word *look* really sounded like a word, but I think he said something like, "Look what I've got."

"Hey, your TV!"

They nodded, and Dad busied himself setting it up on top of my desk. I could see it perfectly from my bed.

Mom handed me the *TV Guide* and said, "You can see what's on." She was sitting on my left side, so I didn't have any trouble getting that sentence.

While Dad fiddled with the rabbit ears and adjusted the picture, I scanned the TV schedule and said, "There's an old 'I Love Lucy' on."

"What channel?" Mom asked.

I told Dad, and he flicked the dial to that station. Soon we were getting caught up in Lucy's antics as, badly sunburned, she tried to model a designer dress.

"Can you hear it?" Mom asked.

"Sort of," I told her, because what I heard was about as little as I'd gotten of Dad's sentence with *look* in it. I still felt as if I had earplugs in, and many of the words sounded so distant or mumbled that I didn't get them at all. But I had seen this particular "Lucy" segment before and didn't have any trouble following the story. "It's okay," I added.

After the show was over, Mom and Dad left my room. Dad had handed me the remote control, so I kept changing the channels until I found the "Twilight Zone." It was a weekday morning, and my choices were oldies, game shows, or soaps.

The theme music came through in a tinny way, but my heart sank when the program began. Whereas "Lucy" had seemed okay, this didn't. I had never seen this segment before. The dialogue was all mumbled so that I got bits and pieces that didn't go together well enough to help me understand what was going on. There wasn't much action on the screen either to clue me in. It started to drive me crazy. I tried sitting very still, straining to get some useful sound, but the dialogue might just as well have been in Chinese.

I switched to a game show. The host was reading questions to the contestants, who were supposed to answer. I got only bits and pieces once again and couldn't even play along at home by trying to think of the right answers myself.

I switched the channel again, this time to what looked like a soap opera. Somebody was on the witness stand in court, but I tapped the remote control to *off* in frustration when I couldn't follow this program either.

How could this be happening to me? I felt as if I had dropped through a hole into my own private twilight zone. I felt so alone, closed out even from the dumbest soap opera or game show. I was tired of escaping to Mary, Queen of Scots' day and longed to be part of today's world in the way I'd always been—before. I couldn't even enjoy a little television while I got stronger.

Sara was the first friend I saw after I was home from the hospital. She and her family had been on vacation when I got sick, so Sara didn't know I was sick until after they got back from the Wisconsin Dells.

The visit didn't go very well. Somehow, everything between Sara and me was changed. For one thing, my hearing trouble got in the way; I had to ask her to repeat everything she said. I worked at getting her words any way I could, mostly through a combination of watching her lips, using what little hearing I still had, and gritting my teeth to stay very watchful and patient. But straining so hard to get what she was saying made me feel very tense. I felt like crying. Being with my best friend now was so different. I was trying so hard, and Sara looked ready to walk out.

"What really happened to you?" she asked, mouthing the words like you do when you want to ask somebody something through a rolled up car window. It was obvious somebody, probably either her mom or mine, had said something to her about my hearing. She was also talking just a bit more slowly than usual.

I told her about the day of the headache and having meningitis.

"Yeah, Mom said you had meningitis. She said it can be deadly." She emphasized *deadly* as though it was her mom's word, and then she gave the universal finger-slitting-the-throat gesture. When I didn't say anything right away, she added, although I had to have her repeat it twice, "I thought meningitis usually killed people."

"Sometimes it does," I told her, supplying the definition of *meningitis* that I'd memorized from a dictionary: *inflammation of the meninges, or the membranes that enclose the brain and spinal cord*. In other words, it really can be deadly, and I was lucky to be alive.

When my words came out, I said, "I was lucky . . . I guess."

I felt embarrassed when I had to ask Sara to repeat what she'd said again. She had forgotten and talked in her old familiar mile-a-minute way.

"Why did you say 'I guess,' Gustie? Aren't you glad to still be alive?"

Would I have been better off dead? I was beginning to wonder. I couldn't even walk unless someone helped me. I looked like a string bean because I was down to 82 pounds, much too little for my 5'4" frame, and I had bluish circles under my eyes. Whenever I thought of school starting soon, I cried. I knew that I wouldn't be well enough to be there the first day. So there I was, straining for small talk with my best friend, wondering if I'd ever talk normally with people again. I was glad to be alive, I decided, but I wanted more than anything else in the world to be the old me. But how could I explain this to another person? Everything was still so confusing to me.

"I don't know why I said that, Sara, I really don't. I guess it's because I'm feeling a little bit sorry for myself. I'm weak, I can't hear right, and I just feel so out of things," I told her honestly, begging silently with my eyes for her old understanding and continued friendship.

When our eyes met, I don't know how to describe what I saw in Sara's. Maybe I was imagining it, but it was like there was a little wall there that shut me out. Then the little wall was gone.

She gave me a warm, Sara-like hug and said, "You'll get better." I didn't get some of the rest, but I think it was "We're all pulling for you, Gustie. You bet we are."

Then, maybe trying to lighten an emotional moment, Sara said something that made me feel awful. It was as if she had finally figured out my situation and had just realized the meaning of my illness and the changes it was making in my life.

"Does this mean you can't be a cheerleader?"

From Sara's expression, you'd have thought not being a cheerleader was the end of the world. Actually, now that I thought of it, it did seem pretty grim. For some reason that I didn't understand, though, I didn't want Sara to know how much it meant to me.

I just said, "That's right. I'll miss you guys."

I changed the subject then. I asked about her vacation and stuff. Sara talked freely, but I couldn't always follow her, especially when she talked fast or forgot to look right at me. If I interrupted to ask her to repeat something, she did, but somehow it froze Sara and spoiled our conversation. I could tell talking to me had become a chore more than anything else to Sara.

I realized that I was very tired. Sara hadn't been with me for even a half hour yet.

Before she left, she said, "We're having a last wiener roast tonight on the beach before school starts." Boy, was *wiener* a tough word to get. Sara got the point across by pretending she was chewing and mouthing "bow wow." Then she did an impression of a wienie dog. Watching her act like that made me feel better.

I smiled, wishing her a great time. "Be sure to come back and tell me all about the hot dog roast."

I tried to keep from getting serious again. I wanted, instead, to grab Sara's hand and make that a plea. I felt like saying. *"Please come back, Sara. I feel so left out and want to know what's going on even if I can't be there. I'm still me. Be patient. Right now, I'm tired, frustrated, and very scared. Please don't abandon me."*

But Sara came back only a few times, mainly just to drop off books after school started.

I never did hear about the wienie roast.

Doctors and Tests

·

Gradually, I was getting stronger, but my hearing wasn't getting better. Since the doctors in our town couldn't make it right again, my parents made an appointment for me to see a specialist in Chicago.

I had already seen three ear doctors, and already I didn't like them much. I guess that isn't fair. I'm sure there are different kinds of ear doctors, just like there are different kinds of anything. It's just that the ones I saw poked their instruments with the little lights into my ears, smiled at me, and had their assistants give me hearing tests. I didn't mind the ear exams or the hearing tests. What bothered me was that I was beginning to feel like one big set of ears. The doctors never said much to me. They never told me what was happening beyond "This may feel a little funny," or "Lay your head back against the headrest." Going to their offices and having tests reminded me of a factory assembly line. Didn't anyone care how I felt about all this?

I wanted someone who could tell me if my hearing would get better and what would happen to my life if it didn't. Was I going to be deaf all my life? What did deaf people do? I wanted someone to help me handle my feelings and frustrations every time I tried to enjoy TV and felt shut out when I couldn't understand the actors' words, or when I felt like using the phone and couldn't. I needed help in understanding Sara's coolness toward me. Even my parents didn't seem the same. They sort of hovered over me and were always antsy. Sometimes I felt that people saw me as either mentally retarded or six years old. To use one of Gram's favorite words, too many people were pussyfooting around. They just didn't act like they used to.

Anyway, this guy in Chicago, Dr. Wilfred Gleaves, was supposed to be, as my parents said, *eminent*. A big wheel. Mom, Dad, and I went together to see him that first time. Dad drove, and Mom and I tried to make our usual small talk as we rode along the Indiana Toll Road. Our previous trips to Chicago had been such fun, but everything fell flat this time. It kind of hurt to remember.

One time we saw *The Nutcracker* at McCormick Place. Another time we watched the beautiful Lippizaner stallions jump high and do their famous dancelike steps. Lots of times we went to Chicago around Christmas to see all the lights along Michigan Avenue and the huge Christmas tree in the Walnut Room at Marshall Field's. Then, we'd go hear the carillon at the Tribune Tower play carols. I choked up thinking about the carols. I didn't know if I'd be able to hear any this Christmas.

Mom's mind was also on the past. She turned around and said, "Do you remember the tickle bridge?

"Yes," I answered, remembering. The "tickle bridge" had a funny hump in it that made you feel like you were on a small roller coaster. Normally, we didn't go over it because we took the Chicago Skyway, but one time Dad wanted to drive to Chicago the old way. He remembered how it was before they built the toll road and skyway.

My mind was more on my iffy future and the ear doctor than on the tickle bridge, though. I smiled at Mom and said, "I remember." Then I changed the subject by asking, "Mom, Dad, what's Dr. Gleaves going to be like?"

Dad was driving, so he couldn't turn his head for me to see his mouth or get the full benefit of his voice. Mom answered for both of them.

"Dad says that Dr. Gleaves is elderly, Gustie, and he is one of the best ear doctors in the country."

I didn't get Mom's sentence in one nice, orderly piece. I stumbled over the word *elderly,* so Mom used a different word.

I noticed that Mom and Dad didn't look tense. For maybe the first time since I got sick, they looked almost like normal. And that scared me. They were, I realized right there in the car, filled with hope; they, too, wanted, the old me back. I felt that I had no control over my life because how it turned out depended on my dumb ears.

Mom said a little more about Dr. Gleaves, but it was hard to keep my mind on what she said. The background noise of the traveling car was irritating because it interfered with the sound of Mom's voice. Trying to understand her sentences was really tiring. In fact, I was getting a headache from watching Mom like a hawk and straining superhard to hear her voice. If I stopped to look at something along the highway, I knew I'd miss what she said, but sometimes I had to look away. Having to watch so closely made my eyes feel like they'd cross forever. I liked the way Mom substituted words to help me understand, but I also felt increasingly upset. It just didn't seem fair to have to struggle so hard for what was easy for everyone else.

"I hope he's nice," was all I said, adding to myself the hope that he could fix me up.

Then we were silent again. My thoughts drifted from the upcoming visit with the new doctor back to last week and the day school started after summer vacation. I couldn't be there. I felt pretty sorry for myself when I pictured Sara, Dana, and the rest of the group in their new Calvins—jeans I would have shopped for with them if I hadn't gotten sick. I felt like ripping off my pajamas.

Not only was my hearing all messed up, but my balance was too. Dad had explained to me that the menigitis had also affected my balance mechanism, which is located in the ears. It was weird. I could walk, but I had to think hard about taking each step; sometimes I had to put my arms straight out from my sides, kind of like a tightrope walker, to keep from teetering and falling over. Just walking around the house I had the sensation of being on a rocking boat or just coming off a wild carnival ride because the ground felt like it was moving. Handling the stairs at school would have been murder, and I wasn't sure what would happen if I got bumped. I might fall flat on my face.

Anyway, the big three—my hearing, my balance, and the weakness from having been so sick—kept me out of school. Maybe that sounds like fun, but I didn't like it because I felt so cut off.

"I want to be there," I whispered to my cat.

Then Mom came into my room and said, "How would you like a little company after school?"

I perked up a little. "That'd be great. Who?"

"Sara and Dana," she said, smiling as if she'd pulled a white rabbit out of a hat.

"Great."

Then, because I felt sort of scrungy, I asked Mom to fix my hair and help me clean up a little. By the time we'd done that, I was really worn out, but I looked better.

Mom had just plumped up my pillows and draped me against them when she said, "_____."

"Huh?"

"Doorbell," she repeated, pointing off in the direction of the front door.

"Oh."

She left to answer the door while I took a gulp of water and tried to look just a teeny bit like Garbo. Rag doll was probably closer to the truth.

"Here they are," Mom said, or at least her gesture of ushering Sara and Dana in made me think that was what she said. She seemed to be talking from the next room, not from just a few feet away.

"Hi, Gustie," my friends said as Dana handed me something wrapped in shiny green paper. She said something that I missed.

"Sit down," I said, patting the edge of my bed. Then, beginning to ease apart the paper where it was stapled together, I told Dana, "This looks interesting." I didn't hear the paper rustle as I pulled it away.

Holding up a ceramic frog vase with a plant in it, I said, "Oh, thank you, Dana. It's so cute. I really like it." Since all my hospital flowers had withered, I was glad to have a plant. I knew I could count on

Mom's green thumb to make it last a long time.

I reached over and put the plant on top of my bedside lamp table.

Nobody said anything for a few seconds, and then we all started talking at the same time:

"Tell me about . . ." I started.

"Here are your . . ." Sara said.

"_____," Dana began. Hers was garbled.

We all laughed.

"You first," I told Sara, who had held out an armful of school books. I saw a comp book, a French text, a Latin book, and a fat one that was probably for history.

"This should keep me busy," I groaned, but I was secretly pleased to have this evidence that I was still a part of Central. About the worst thing I could think of was not to advance with the rest of my class.

"Gustie, _____ teachers _____ paper," Sara said.

Understanding her was sort of like a fill-in-the-blanks test. I wanted very much, for some reason, not to have to ask Sara and Dana to do a lot of repeating. At first, I didn't know what Sara meant, but then I began using my eyes. I figured out what she'd probably said when I noticed papers sticking out of the top of each book. As Sara placed the stack on the bed near me, I opened the comp book and verified my guess that the papers were assignment sheets from each teacher.

"Thanks," I told her.

"_____," Dana said, taping the comp book.

Feeling confident after having guessed right with Sara and making use of the phrase *same book* in Dana's partly understood sentence, I decided that she must be comparing this book with last year's comp book.

"It looks different to me," I commented.

"No, Gustie," put in Sara, "Dana said, '_____ got dray _____ same book.'"

It didn't make sense. Suddenly my heart seemed to be racing. Not understanding made me feel so stupid.

"Oh, I see," I bluffed, too embarrassed to ask either one of them to repeat. Much later, I learned that Dana had Mr. Drayton for English, instead of Mrs. Zenor, but that she had the same comp book that Sara and I had in the other class.

"Thanks again for bringing them," I told them, patting the pile of books.

Then, deciding to talk before they could throw in anymore fill-in-the-blanks sentences at me, I asked, "Well, how did the first day back go?"

I surveyed their new jeans, worn with summer T-shirts that really set off their tans. My tan had faded to pasty white, and I envied their good health. Noticing my white arms, I remembered that I'd been a deep tan too last September when school began. Everything was unbelievably different at the start of this school year.

"Cindy broke up with _____," Sara told me.

"Who?" I couldn't resist asking. I was sure she had said Jeff, the name of the guy Cindy had been bonkers over the last time I saw her, and I couldn't imagine them breaking up.

"_____ going _____ Robert _____."

"Robert Schmidt?" I asked. Even though I'd missed most of that sentence, fortunately I'd gotten the crucial name Robert. But I didn't feel any sense of accomplishment. My spirits took a nose dive, in fact, because I felt so out of things. When had Cindy's break-up happened? Nobody had mentioned it to me before; I used to always hear about those things right away either from Sara or Dana. What else had been going on while I'd been in bed?

It suddenly dawned on me that I'd been so busy trying to hear, trying to walk again, and trying to hang in there until I got better that I'd almost forgotten that other people were just going on about their business.

"Umm hmm," it looked like both of my friends said in answer to my guess about Robert Schmidt.

I wanted to know everything now.

"What about you two?" I tried to ask casually, even though I desperately wanted the lowdown on their love lives, unrequited or real.

26

"It's _____ world," Sara said. "_____ tied _____."
"_____ awful," Dana added.

They were talking very fast now, and although I wanted to tell them to wait and let me catch up, I let them move away from me like an engine chugging faster and faster. They didn't seem to know that their train had left without me; they were talking back and forth to each other now, forgetting that I wasn't like I used to be. I let them go because suddenly I was too tired to keep trying.

Mom's arm waving before my face broke my reverie.

"We're here," she said as we pulled into the garage. My ears popped like they always had in elevators as we made our way up to Dr. Gleaves's nineteenth floor office. We stepped into a pretty waiting room with lettuce green carpeting and yellow-cushioned wicker furniture. It reminded me of a patio or sunroom.

The pleasant room didn't make waiting easy, though. I flipped the pages of one magazine after another and watched patients coming and going. It was odd how so many of them were old. I wondered if I'd turn into an "old" person if my hearing didn't get better. I didn't know anyone my age who was deaf, and I didn't see any kids or teenagers in the waiting room.

I won't bore you with details. Dr. Gleaves didn't do much on my first visit. He was tall and kind of skinny and didn't have much hair. He asked my parents questions about my medical history and progress since I had had meningitis. Then he took me into a room with a dentist's-type chair and examined my ears with several instruments. I don't know what he saw, but every once in a while he said "Mmm" and that was it.

I had just one hearing test that day. It was in a sound-proofed closet-sized room. I wore headphones and raised my finger every time I heard a tone. Some tones were very shrill and others were more a deep rumble that I felt rather than heard. I don't think I heard as many tones as when I'd had the same test in my hometown. In fact, the test confirmed that I had no hearing at all in my right ear.

After the hearing test, my first appointment with Dr. Gleaves was over. For the next few weeks, we went back to Chicago each Tuesday for more tests. The doctor also had me on some medicine. It turned out not to help me, but I guess it was worth a try.

I had this one test over and over again, and I hated it each time. It probably has a real name, but I call it the Say the Word test. A voice— I don't know if it was on a record or somebody I couldn't see—would say, "Say the word _____." I was supposed to fill in the blank with the word that had just been said. Often the voice was loud enough for me to hear, but the words came through strangely, like, "Say the word *tootbruss*." More often, what I heard was, "Say the word *G*$%@#)+*." It was just jumbled sound that I couldn't turn into a word no matter how hard I tried. There were also little "holes" in the test when I heard nothing at all; I wondered if the record was still playing, only in quiet tones that I couldn't hear.

I got very tired of so many tests. I wouldn't have minded any of them if the doctors had helped me to hear better, but in a strange way, my hearing was both better and worse than it had been before. If that seems confusing to you, it was a lot more so for me.

Not long after my first appointment with Dr. Gleaves, something really odd began happening with my hearing. Up until that time I had heard sound as if I'd had a bad telephone connection or earplugs in my ears—the words came through only here and there all the time. Suddenly my hearing began going way up and down like a yo-yo.

One advantage of the changing hearing was that on the good days I could hear almost everything someone said, especially if the person sat close to me and there weren't a lot of background noises. I could even hear a lot of the dialogue on TV.

But on other days I was practically deaf—no mumbles even—no matter how hard I strained to hear. I couldn't help but wonder if my hearing would zoom down one day and stay that way forever, like a yo-yo sometimes plunks to the end of its string and won't come back up.

The yo-yoing made problems for me. I mean, who was I anyway?

It's as if there was a hearing me and a deaf me, and I never knew which me I'd be when I woke up in the morning. It got so that I saw my life in terms of "good" days and "bad" days.

On a good day, I was more like my old self before I had meningitis. Even then, I didn't hear as well as I used to before I got sick, but it wasn't too bad. I could even use the phone on those days. Although there were words that I missed in any conversation, and even though the voices sounded tinny and different, I could carry on a decent phone conversation if I remembered to put my good ear to the receiver.

A bad day made me very depressed and scared. I had to admit to myself then that I had a serious problem that might never go away. It might even get worse. Those were the days when I couldn't hear much at all. I felt shut out because I couldn't talk with people without trying superhard to get their end of the conversation. I'd strain with all my might, but I just couldn't pick up any sound that would help me understand.

On the bad days, the phone was useless. If I managed to hear any voice tones at all—and usually I didn't—there just weren't any words that came through. I might as well have been wearing extra-thick earmuffs.

I can't describe my feeling of helplessness when the phone rang on a bad day and I knew Sara or someone else was as close as the phone, only not for me. I'd taken calling people and being called for granted, and now I realized in a new way what an important part of life that particular link with others is. My link had rusted away.

On the bad days I felt separated from the chain of routine happenings. I wanted to talk about this with my parents, but it seemed impossible. They tried to act as if nothing had changed at home. They must have thought they did a good job of hiding their worry from me, but I could see it. Dad has this funny little wrinkle right between the eyebrows that always gets deeper when he is tired or worried. Lately, it had been looking like the Grand Canyon. Meanwhile, Mom often gave me her poor-little-baby smile.

I wanted to comfort them, to tell them that everything would be okay, but how could I do that when I wasn't sure it really would work out? I also worried that if I told them my fears about the future, they'd just feel worse.

When I brought it up anyway, they acted fakey, like parents sometimes do when they want you to think everything is okay but it really isn't. And that made me mad and even more scared. Did they know something awful?

A conversation would go something like this, only of course in a real conversation, I had to ask for them to do lots of repeating if it was a bad day of hearing:

"Dad, am I going to lose more hearing?"

"Well, honey, you know that's not my specialty. We can hope for the best."

"But what do my doctors say?"

"These things are so complicated. Yes, you could lose more, but why worry about something that may never happen?"

"Maybe it's better to face it head-on."

Mom would pipe in with something like, "Think positively, Gustie."

Ironically, sometimes I'd miss a sentence like that and then realize that it was almost impossible to think positively when I'd had to ask her to repeat the sentence four times. I know she meant well, but it only made me feel more frustrated. Besides, wishful thinking wouldn't make my ears right.

"But I need to know what to expect. Don't I have a right to know? I need to try to get ready for whatever might happen. This is my life we're talking about."

"Trust us to know what's best," one of them might advise, closing the subject.

They made me feel like a baby. I had a hard time trusting them because of some of their actions.

One day, for example, I walked into the living room and saw a bare wall where our spinet piano had been ever since I could remember. Mom was engrossed in a book, but I interrupted her anyway.

"Where's the piano?" I asked. "Did it need to be fixed?"

"Uh, no," she said, looking as if she really wanted to just go on reading the thick novel. "Dad and I saw the most beautiful velvet couch that'll be so perfect there. It's . . ."

"Oh come on, that's not it," I interrupted with an awful suspicion starting to panic me. Then I put the suspicion into words, "You sold it! You did, didn't you?"

Mom's expression said she had. I don't know if I felt angrier at their selling it or at the look of pity Mom gave me just then.

"How could you do that, Mom? I love that piano."

"Yes, you did love it, and you played like an angel."

"Do you think I've suddenly forgotten everything I knew before I got sick?" I asked more calmly than I felt. My whole life seemed to be in the past tense, just like the verbs in Mom's sentence.

"No," she admitted, "but you hadn't touched the piano since you came home from the hospital. Dad and I thought . . ."

"Dad and you thought!" I interrupted again. Boy, was I fuming now. "What about me, Mom? True, I haven't played since I was sick, but I haven't done lots of things yet. I haven't even gone back to school," I reminded her.

Mom and I ended up in tears. Although I could tell she felt terrible and she apologized for the piano sale, Mom and Dad still could not talk about their feelings about my illness and hearing. Their strained looks continued. We just didn't communicate.

I felt awful, like I'd spoiled their lives by getting sick.

Back To School

·

In the middle of October, on a day of good hearing, I went back to school. I'd come a long way since I'd needed help just to walk to the bathroom. I was still taking hearing tests and medical exams, I still got tired easily, and my balance wasn't as good as it had been before I was sick, so I went back for just two classes. I would add more as I got stronger.

Thanks to Mom, I'd done pretty well keeping up with all my school work at home. Although she had arranged for Sara to drop off my books that first day of school after summer vacation, Mom had taken over that chore by going to Central once or twice a week to get my assignments, turn in my papers, and so forth. Under her supervision, I was even allowed to take tests at home.

Without assignments to bring me regularly, Sara's visits had tapered off to almost none. Although she had called, it usually was on the bad days when I hadn't been able to hear her. The times I'd called her, either she wasn't home or her line was busy. I guessed that as school settled into its fall pace, my friends had gotten busier and busier. One reason I looked forward to returning to school was that I missed seeing everyone, especially Sara.

As much as I'd been wanting to be at school, though, I had mixed feelings now that I was actually going back. At home, I could stop studying when I got tired, and I didn't have to worry about hearing teachers and other students. I didn't have any idea how much I'd be able to get in class, even on the good days, and I didn't know how my teachers would react when all of a sudden I came back. Would everyone stare at me? Would my balance make me look drunk? Would I become a school joke? Would my friends want to talk to me if they had to repeat things? I didn't even know for sure if the work I'd been doing at home was enough to make me caught up, or if the teachers had maybe given me easier assignments because they felt sorry for me. Would I end up behind all semester?

I'd soon find out.

As I walked under the arched main doorway of Central, I thought how strange it was that the school hadn't changed a bit while my whole life had. It was sort of like the mortar holding my life together had crumbled and changed the shape of the present and my entire future.

To my relief, everybody at school seemed glad to see me. There were lots of "Welcome backs!"

Something was different, though. Even though it was a day of good hearing, I wasn't prepared for the difficulties I found. The din of slamming locker doors and yells and other noises really got in the way of my understanding speech in the halls.

Although it hadn't taken any powers of concentration to understand and respond to the "hi's," I had trouble with Cindy. When she ran up to me and hugged me, I could tell she'd said something during the hug. I was aware of her voice, but I couldn't hear the words. It's as if all the background sounds in the hall snatched and absorbed the words. When we pulled apart, I asked, "What? I didn't hear what you just said."

Although now I could see her face when she spoke, I got a blank:
"_____."

It was so good to see her, she of the cute nose, that I didn't think twice about asking if she'd repeat it.

She looked embarrassed, though, which in turn embarrassed me.

When she told me "Never mind" and I did hear that, I felt really cut off and alone there in the hall with all those people milling around.

When Cindy looked at her watch and scampered down the hall after a quick good-bye, I realized that I'd better get to Mrs. Zenor's room for my English class. I wanted to sort of feel things out with her before the rest of the class arrived and made it impossible.

Fortunately, my locker was just a few steps away from the classroom, so I didn't have to worry much about my balance in getting there. I had my books carefully balanced in the crook of one arm and my purse counterbalanced over the other shoulder, but I didn't know if I'd be able to keep from falling if someone bumped me hard. To offset any problems of that kind, I walked very close to the wall. I really felt self-conscious about hugging the wall that way, but I knew it was better than possibly going sprawling. At least concentrating on walking to class took my mind off the disappointment of Cindy's embarrassment with me.

Mrs. Zenor was waiting in the room when I walked in, but most of the students hadn't yet arrived.

"Hello there," she told me, walking right over to me as I entered. As she moved closer, I realized that she was shouting at me, no doubt believing it would help. Her raised voice just made my good ear tingle uncomfortably, but I couldn't think of a polite way to tell her to quiet down, so I didn't say anything.

"Gustie, your work has been superb."

Even with the sound of her voice ringing in my ear, I felt enormously relieved to have her compliment me on my work. Maybe the teachers had given me the regular homework after all, so I wouldn't be behind.

"Thank you," I told her as I handed her a composition I'd finished just yesterday. She glanced at it and rolled it lengthwise into a tube.

"How do you feel about being back?" she asked.

"I'm really glad to be here, Mrs. Zenor."

"Good. If you have any problems at all, please let me know." Then she jerked her head up, looked past me, and said, "Oh, there's Mr.

Harley." Glancing over my shoulder, I noticed the science teacher standing in the doorway. "We'll talk more after class if you need to," she told me. I nodded.

As Mrs. Zenor walked toward Mr. Harley, I looked around the room and saw that it had about twenty-five chairs in it. Mom had given me a pep talk about sitting in the front so that I could get the full benefit of Mrs. Zenor's voice. I chose a front row chair that was slightly on the right side of the room to keep my good ear in the best position for hearing.

Just as I sat down, Sara walked in. She looked so, I don't know, Sara-like. When I saw her familiar figure coming into the room, I felt a wave of love for the friend who had been like a sister to me, and I realized more than ever how much I'd missed the kind of regular togetherness we'd had before I got sick.

"Hi, Gustie," she called.

"Hi. Do you want to sit up here with me?" I asked, patting the chair to my left. We'd always sat beside each other in the classes where we'd had a choice, so my question was just a formality.

"I will for just a minute," she told me, "but I already have a seat next to Marcia Trent."

Marcia Trent? That was news to me. Sara had never especially liked Marcia, who ran with a faster crowd than our group. I was hurt that Sara didn't want to get right back into our old habit of sitting together, but I told myself that sooner or later she'd be back beside me and that took some of the sting away.

Now, coming to sit beside me for a minute before Mrs. Zenor came back into the room, Sara said, "How are you doing, Gustie? You look awfully thin."

Actually, I was up to ninety pounds from the eighty-two I'd been for a while, and I felt that I looked pretty good. I tried telling myself that a woman can never be too rich or too thin, but I didn't quite believe it when I saw Sara's eyes flick over my scrawny body.

I noticed that I was hearing Sara's voice very well. Maybe it was because the room was still quiet and it was such a good day of hearing.

Mentally comparing it to the weeks when I felt like I'd worn the same pair of earplugs day after day, I thought the bad days now were almost worth it just to understand this well on the few really good days.

"I'm so glad to be back." Then, reaching over to lightly brush the top of her hand, I added, "I can hardly wait to get together so you can fill me in on what's been going on."

"I'll call you later," she said.

Oh no, not that dumb phone again. I knew that the phone was practically grafted onto Sara's ear when she was home, but it's not as if there weren't alternatives to the telephone. We'd see each other in this class five days a week, for one thing. I decided to be open about my phone problem right then and there.

"Sara, some days I just can't hear well enough to use the phone," I told her, intending to give her a nutshell account of the up-down hearing, but Mrs. Zenor came back into the room just then, and everybody scurried to their chairs.

Sara mumbled something that was lost as chairs scraped the floor and books were dropped onto chair arms or the floor. She moved to a seat two rows behind me. Turning slightly, I could see her giggling with Marcia. "*That used to be me next to Sara*," I thought, and I felt an awful tightening in my chest. Even more than I had a few minutes ago with Cindy, I felt shut out and alone. I took a deep breath and tried to concentrate just on hearing the teacher.

Mrs. Zenor embarrassed me by making a big show of my return to school. "Class," she began in a very loud voice that made a kid near me shake his head exaggeratedly and pound it with the heal of his hand. "Gustie Blaine is back with us after her ordeal with encephalitis." "*Wrong illness*," I amended silently. "She has a slight hearing problem but has kept up with the work at home. Let's all welcome Gustie back."

Then they all clapped, and my embarrassment left in the flood of pleasure brought by being welcomed back.

Once the actual class began, Mrs. Zenor no longer shouted or stood next to me as she spoke. I could hear her normal voice tones quite well, and actually it was a relief not to have her voice ringing in my ear.

I was at a disadvantage in class that day, though, because we were grading each other's papers. The assignment had been to read the sentences in the textbook exercise and choose the right verb; for example, "Sandra and Michael were (*laying, lying*) on the warm sand." We were going around the class with each of us taking the next sentence as our turn came.

My heart sank as Mrs. Zenor began by calling on a student way across the room. I couldn't hear him clearly enough to understand. Maybe I should have expected it, but this was such a good day of hearing that I really had not counted on any problems. Once again, I felt very cut off, especially when I noticed kids around the room goofing off and not listening. It just seemed to drive home the fact that even if I paid attention, I didn't have much choice in the matter of listening or not. When I did hear a sentence, sometimes the verbs were so similar that my messed-up hearing couldn't quite tell the difference between the two key words.

Fortunately, the lesson was easy for me. I felt confident that I could grade Terry Morgan's paper on my own, even if I didn't hear everything. I was tense, though, knowing my sentence would come up sooner or later. Instead of worrying, like some students did, about giving the wrong verb, I was worried that I'd read the wrong *sentence*. It was weird.

"Gustie?" Mrs. Zenor said, breaking into my thoughts.

Oh no! Was I going to have to say "What?" I felt so nervous; I could tell my heart was racing, and my hands were shaking just a tiny bit. As I twisted my amethyst ring, I realized that I didn't want to reveal that I hadn't heard everything. I also didn't want everybody to feel sorry for me. But Mrs. Zenor saved me this time.

"Would you please read number nineteen for us?" she asked me. Although she had forgotten to shout, I heard her just fine.

Immediately relaxing, I read my sentence correctly and felt like taking a bow. I knew that was stupid, but for a while I had been sure I'd look like a dunce and read a sentence that had just been done.

Soon after that, class was over. Everybody, including Sara huddled close to Marcia Trent, was pouring out of the room. Although I hadn't really been aware of making the decision, I stayed for just a minute after class.

"Gustie?" Mrs. Zenor asked, and her smile encouraged me to talk.

"Umm," I began weakly, but then I dove right in. "I had trouble hearing the students reading the exercises. I think maybe, if it's all right, someone should grade the paper I'd normally check over. Although I didn't have trouble with this lesson, when we come to ones I'm not as sure about, I don't think I can rely on myself to always hear the right answer or know it on my own."

As I'd spoken, her features had drawn together into a look of mild surprise. Although of course she'd known about my hearing loss, I guessed that my understanding her so well, even when she forgot to shout, had led her to the conclusion that I wouldn't have much of a problem hearing the students either.

Everything was okay, though. "No problem at all, Gustie," she responded. "Someone can easily grade two papers."

That made me glad I'd jumped right in and explained the problem. I left the room feeling pretty good about my first class back at school.

Just as I'd been doing with life in general, I began to divide school into good days and bad days, according to how well I could hear.

On good hearing days, classes went about like the first day in Mrs. Zenor's English class. I noticed that I could fake understanding a lot of the time to make other people feel that I hadn't changed much. I was just Gustie with a little hearing problem, and everybody seemed more comfortable around me then. I could almost even convince myself that I was the old me.

The bad days were empty and lonely enough, but the way people acted around me on those days made me feel even worse. Instead of being Gustie, it seemed like they thought of me as "The Deaf Girl." I felt like a failure on the bad days for provoking their impatience.

I tried hard to figure out what they were thinking. Some people were too polite, too smiley, and a little bit stiff, sort of like people sometimes are if a person's a bore or has a bad case of BO. Who knows? Maybe some of my friends were even afraid that they could catch my hearing loss the way people catch the flu.

On the bad hearing days, sitting in class was even worse than watching television with no sound, so Mom sometimes let me stay home on those days. I'd sleep a lot then just to escape, hoping that I'd hear better when I woke up.

The yo-yoing, which I finally learned from Dad is called fluctuation, made another kind of problem: Other people often couldn't understand how my hearing could change so drastically—up, down, up, down, etc.

On one of the good days at school, for example, I had a very upsetting experience. I was on my way to the library, chanting *"right, left, right, left,"* to myself as I walked because I still had to concentrate on putting one foot in front of the other. I suddenly heard Sara's voice from around a tall clump of bushes. My hearing was as high as 80% that day, which, I'd learned from tests, was about the top for me. That's pretty good hearing, so I could hear Sara without much straining, especially since it was after school and there wasn't much background noise. She wasn't trying to keep her voice down anyway.

I wished she had. I wouldn't have listened in, but then I heard my name and felt frozen there behind the bushes, which screened us from each other.

". . . Gustie in class," Sara was saying to someone I hadn't yet identified. "_____ teacher's pet _____ can't hear right, and you know what?"

Maybe another voice said "What?"

"I think she fakes it sometimes."

What! I almost charged around the bushes to confront Sara. What a horrible accusation. It made me feel even worse than the unfair teacher's pet label.

Then I heard another voice ask, "What do you mean?" It was Dana, raising her voice a little.

"She can hear better than she lets on."

"Why would anyone do that, Sara especially Gustie?"

There was a pause.

"How would I know. For attention _____." Haven't you noticed the way _____ sometimes hears you and sometimes doesn't? _____ convenient. _____ stays home from school when she isn't really sick. It's like she's using a very minor problem. _____ a whole lot better than she lets on."

I don't know what Dana answered. I'd heard enough—too much! I felt this awful choking in my throat and burning behind my eyes. Why didn't Sara ask me about my hearing? Why didn't she let me or my parents explain the fluctuation? I'd tried to make plans with her several times since I'd returned to school, but she'd always been "too busy." Why would this friend of so many years—*my best friend*—talk like that about me? I didn't have any answers.

If pride hadn't kept me from demanding some answers from Sara, I would have confronted her right then and there, but I had started to cry and didn't want her to see how deeply hurt I felt. I carried the hurt home and cried into Jasmine's soft fur.

School was also rough because some of my teachers didn't seem to understand my situation. Mr. Armour, my French teacher, was the worst.

After a few weeks back at school I was definitely feeling stronger. In fact, I felt strong enough to return to French class. I'd already added Latin, so French would round out my school day to four classes.

I really liked French; this would be my second year of it. I had had some daydreams about becoming a translator, but I guessed I wouldn't be able to now. Anyway, French class that first day back was okay, I thought, even if I didn't hear everything during the oral drills. I had kept up with the vocabulary at home.

I had no way of knowing that Mr. Armour was about to drop a bombshell. It came in the form of a crisply folded note that he handed to me toward the end of class. It read:

Mademoiselle Blaine,

Last year you were one of my most industrious students. It is with regret, then, that I am recommending a waiver of the foreign language requirement in your case.

It is, of course, impossible for you now to speak the language and reach the next level of mastery.

I trust that you are seeking proper medical care that may spare you an impoverished life of total silence, and I sincerely hope that you will have a happy life with other deaf-mutes, despite this tragedy.

(Signed) M. Armour

After reading the note, I just sat there at my desk in the empty classroom and stared at the piece of paper. I felt so many things: shock, anger, humiliation, frustration, and an almost overwhelming fear. Would my life be impoverished? *Impoverished!* Would I become mute? Would they stick me away somewhere in an institution? Every little doubt and fear I'd tried to hide came bubbling to the surface, and a flood of tears started raining down my cheeks in hot little splashes.

The nitty-gritty of it was that Mr. Armour was telling me that I, a straight-A French student, had changed so much that I no longer belonged in his class. Well, maybe that was true, but whatever happened to chances to prove yourself? How could he say for sure what I could or couldn't do?

Did he mean I couldn't go to college? Couldn't get a decent job? Drive a car? Or do a million other things that other people do?

Did Mr. Armour know I'd never be able to learn new words and "reach the next level of mastery" in my very own language?

Would I forget how to talk? Worst of all, would I be a freak? That note hurt me for a long time.

I began to wonder what all my teachers were thinking. Did they feel sorry for me? Were they watching and expecting me to fail? Would they, too, suddenly stick a note into my hand that told me I didn't belong? Latin, because it was another foreign language, worried me the most. I was afraid that even though Miss Hartman was nice and understanding, her reaction might be like Mr. Armour's and she'd suggest I drop out. I didn't want to.

On the day I got Mr. Armour's note, I was tempted to scurry out of Latin class like a timid mouse. But I stayed. I needed to talk to Miss Hartman. It would be better to know how she felt, I told myself.

I felt less sure of myself as the other students filed out of the room. Suddenly, Miss Hartman and I were the only ones left, and wouldn't you know that I felt speechless? Fortunately, she made me feel comfortable.

"I know that Latin must be hard for you now," she said, "but I'm glad you're giving it a good try. You're doing very well."

My hearing was very good that day. We sat close to each other, and there were no distracting background noises, so I could hear her fine.

"Thank you," I told her. Maybe there was hope after all. "You're so understanding." I paused and then once again felt the sting of Mr. Armour's note as I added, "Not everyone is." Suddenly, I started to cry.

Noticing my tears, she asked me to tell her what was wrong. I hadn't planned to, but I ended up telling her about Mr. Armour's note. I even let her read it when she asked me if she could see it.

Miss Hartman is a tiny woman with curly black hair framing a heart-shaped face. As she read the note, her dark eyes began to blaze. I'm not kidding. It looked like little flickers of fire danced in them.

Handing the note back to me, she said, "I can't believe this! Let me speak to that . . . to Mr. Armour on your behalf."

Miss Hartman's offer to help made me feel good, but I wasn't even sure I wanted to be in that class. I still felt really hurt and turned off by his note. Who wants to be around someone who feels you don't belong?

I told Miss Hartman that I wasn't sure I wanted to stay in French.

"Well," she said, "let's let it rest for a few days. Then see how you feel about it. I'll give you my full support if you decide you want to stay in his class. One thing I do know is that you don't need a waiver of the foreign language requirement, Gustie. True, Mr. Armour is the head of the department, but I won't stand for anyone telling me I have to deny a student my class."

I smiled at her offer of support, but then I had a sudden vision of Mr. Armour handing a crisply folded complaint about Miss Hartman to Mr. Forrest, the principal. I felt my smile slip away.

I said, "I don't want you to get into trouble."

She smiled and said, "I won't. This is a matter of humanity more than anything else. There are also antidiscrimination laws."

Her understanding seemed almost too good to be true.

"Miss Hartman?"

"Yes?" she asked, her eyes softening as she looked at me. The little flames in them were gone.

"Does this mean you think I should stay in Latin?" I also briefly explained the hearing fluctuation to make sure that she realized I was having an especially good day and usually didn't hear this well.

She even seemed to understand that.

"Why, of course you should, Gustie," she said as she took one of my hands. "I can't tell you your grades will be as high as last year's. I can't tell you the level of mastery you'll achieve. Maybe foreign language is folly for a hearing-impaired person. To be honest, I just don't know. But, Gustie, let's give it a good try. Don't write off anything without giving it a fair chance."

I squeezed her hand and looked down at my Nikes. I was starting to cry again, only this time my tears had a smile in them because I felt touched by something warm and good. I guess it was the "milk of human kindness" Gram sometimes talked about. One Miss Hartman could make ten Mr. Armours bearable.

"I'm sorry I'm crying," I told her as I reached up to brush away a tear. "All I can say, Miss Hartman, is that what you've just said means the world to me. Thanks. I want to try."

"You're very welcome. But," she added, "I want something in return."

She looked every inch the stern teacher just then. I was almost afraid to ask what she wanted.

"What is it?" I asked. I could feel my heart pounding.

"I want you to be honest and tell me what you get out of class. You may never benefit as you used to from class discussion and oral language drills. Try, but don't knock yourself out. There are alternatives to my grading system, Gustie. I don't have to grade you on oral work. Some of my other students might envy you that, but I'll give you plenty of written exercises."

We had to cut our conversation short because the next class was beginning to come into the room. I think we were about done talking anyway.

"We can talk again, any time you want to. Let me know what you decide to do about French," she told me.

"Thank you so much, Miss Hartman." *Thank you* seemed like such a weak phrase for what I felt. I wanted to hug her.

"Keep your chin up."

I went home that day feeling better about everything.

H.À.

I didn't feel better for long. My hearing started going up and down like crazy. It seemed weird and scary not to know if I'd wake up in the morning and be able to hear as well as I had with Miss Hartman that day after class or be practically deaf.

Lots of people think of peace and quiet as being the same thing, but let me tell you, it wasn't peaceful to be practically deaf. Even though I was always on guard not to miss things, I did miss a lot, expecially in conversations or at school. And, there wasn't anything peaceful about wanting to crawl into a hole until a day of better hearing came along.

Quiet wasn't peace. More and more, it was a big zero.

One Saturday morning in early November, I walked into the kitchen for a late breakfast. Since Mom and Dad had already eaten, I ate my Grape-Nuts alone at the table, where I found a note from Mom letting me know that she had gone grocery shopping. I was just aimlessly looking around the room when the brightly colored picture on the wall calendar caught my eye. From where I was sitting, I could also see foil stars calling attention to squares that were the dates of family birthdays and anniversaries. Mom was a cardoholic who sent a card for every big and not-so-big event.

I saw some writing on unstarred calendar squares, but since I couldn't read it from the table, I took my bowl with me over to the calendar to check out this month's happenings. There was a dental appointment for Dad. The Hansons were having a farewell party for

the Edelmans. Then I saw a square with a notation that read: H.A.—
Gustie, 3:00 p.m.

I had a funny feeling when I saw that. Suddenly my Grape-Nuts
tasted like dry cat food. I stopped chewing but managed to swallow
that bite. Then I set my bowl on the counter.

H.A.? What was H.A.? I wondered if it was the initials of still
another ear doctor. I didn't like finding out about it by chance just
because I'd seen Mom's calendar. She could have told me.

As if she'd been given a cue for a stage entrance, Mom opened the
door just then and walked in carrying two large bags of groceries. She
smiled a "hi" and thanked me as I reached over and took one of the
bags.

"Hi, Mom," I said.

She took off her coat and put it over the back of one of the kitchen
chairs.

"*What's new*?" I felt like asking. "*What surprise are you and Dad
springing on me this time*?"

She said something I didn't hear, but when she repeated it, I got
something about ice cream and decided there must be a carton of it in
one of the bags. We both began going through them and putting the
frozen stuff into the freezer.

After we'd put everything away, I walked over by the calendar and
stood just to the side of it.

Mom didn't notice anything wrong. She poured herself a cup of coffee and sat down at the table

"Hi. How are you today?" she asked. I knew she didn't mean that
in just the regular sense. How I was now included what my hearing
was like that day. This particular day it was pretty far down, but Mom
was close to me, and what I didn't hear, I guessed at or tried to see in
her expressions.

"Kind of so-so," I told her. Sitting back down at the table, I asked.
"What's that H.A. on the calendar?"

She looked puzzled.

"H.A.," I said again. "For the eighth of November."

Then, seeming to remember what her notation meant, she smiled and started talking. She seemed to be talking very fast. Was she nervous? Whatever the reason, I didn't understand anything she said.

"I didn't hear you," I told her.

Although she repeated it, this time more slowly, I still didn't have any idea what she'd said. What was the matter with me today? Trying to talk was so tedious that I felt like crawling out of my skin.

"I still didn't hear you," I admitted as I propped my elbows on the table and rested my chin on my fists in defeat. I stared down at the place mat. Why was my hearing so far down?

Mom noticed my problem. She reached for the telephone pad and a pencil. I had mixed feelings about that. Even though I wanted to know what she'd said and what the mysterious "H.A." on the calendar square meant, and although I appreciated her writing it down without looking impatient, it felt pretty cruddy to need written notes from my own mother.

When she'd finished, it read:

For a minute, I'd forgotten my own shorthand on the calendar.
Dad and I made an appointment with a hearing aid counselor for
you.

A hearing aid counselor? I don't know what I'd expected her note to say, but it wasn't this, that's for sure. The subject of a hearing aid had never come up.

"You mean you just called them up and decided all this without even mentioning it to me or asking me how I felt about it?"

The truth was that I wasn't thrilled about the idea of wearing a hearing aid, but right then Mom and Dad's highhandedness upset me more than anything else.

She scribbled a new note:

We're just trying to do all we can to help you, honey.

I knew that, but that didn't keep me from feeling shut out. "You'd help me a lot more if we talked over going to all these places before you drag me off to them. I appreciate all you're doing but, Mom, sometimes you treat me like I'm eight years old, not fifteen. Can't I be a part of big decisions like this? I'm the one with the messed-up ears, the one who'd have to wear the hearing aid, for Pete's sake."

Mom looked startled by what I'd said. She put down her coffee cup, crossed her hands over her chest, and said, "I'm so sorry. Oh, honey, I didn't know you'd feel this way about it." Although I didn't get every word, I understood enough to figure out what she was telling me, and she didn't have to write it down. "We are just trying to help," she added.

I saw that she really meant it, and I felt my tensed muscles relax a little.

I think my voice softened as I said, "I know you do, Mom, but a hearing aid? It's sort of hard to take in." I pictured the one our elderly neighbor had worn before she died. It sometimes whistled, and it had a cord that ran from her ear down to a little box that she wore pinned to her bra.

Mom said something, and when I drew another blank, she used the note pad again to tell me:

I can understand how you feel, but lots of people wear them these days, Gustie, and most of the aids are inconspicuous.

"You mean I wouldn't have to have a cord dangling down to a box inside my bra?"

"You're thinking of Mrs. Raymond, aren't you?" she said. I got the name and figured the rest out. I nodded that I was.

In another note she wrote:

No. Lots of them fit right into the ear or behind the ear. Even the president wears one.

"That's just it, Mom, He's old. Hearing aids are for old folks. I'm only fifteen. Do I have to go to that place?"

She scribbled again:

Not everyone who wears a hearing aid is old, Gustie, and I think it's worth trying.

Would it get rid of the fluctuation that I hated so much? Would I be able to use the phone like before? Hear music again? Talk to my friends and understand what they said to me? Understand in school? Be part of things?

"All right. I'll go," I told her, thinking that anything, even some awful cord dangling into my bra, would be worth it if I could just hear right all the time.

In my room that night, though, I didn't feel so positive about trying a hearing aid.

"Oh, Jasmine, my life is a mess," I told my cat. She reached a paw out and stretched it my way as if sympathizing with me.

Her blue eyes followed my motions as I suddenly grabbed a scarf out of a drawer, turned it into a makeshift shawl, hobbled toward her using an umbrella as a cane, and said, "Dahhling, wait while I adjust my H.A."

Jasmine just stared at me. She didn't seem aware that I had turned myself into an old lady.

I threw off the scarf, stood the umbrella back in its corner, and pulled on a nightgown.

The minute I pulled up the covers, I started to cry. It just wasn't fair. What had I ever done to deserve this? I thought of all those people at Pine Lake last summer, all the people who had eaten at Jacob's—both possible places where I'd been exposed to meningitis. Of all those people, all those hundreds, why me? And why, if I had to get so sick, did my hearing have to be messed up? Whey couldn't I have just gotten well like I did after the chicken pox or the flu? Why, why, why?

Almost as if she sensed my feelings, Jasmine curled up next to me. I put an arm around her and let my tears fall onto her fur. She didn't seem to mind.

"I ought to be getting a new stereo, not a hearing aid," I whispered.

Two days later, something happened to make me feel better again about the idea of getting a hearing aid. Dad brought home a woman who worked in the hospital admitting office. The first thing I noticed about Mrs. Crier was that she could have been a model or an actress; she was beautiful. She had black hair, very large dark eyes, and beautiful olive skin. I guessed she was about twenty-five. I could picture her wearing a Spanish comb and a lace mantilla.

My hearing was so far down that evening that the introductions were made through writing. Since I didn't know Mrs. Crier, and since it was so hard to try to make conversation when my hearing was so bad, I planned to stay just long enough not to be rude. Then, I would make an escape to my room.

But Mom put a hand on my arm in a gesture that said, "No, don't go yet, Gustie."

Dad added something and pointed to me, as if he'd said, "She's here to see you." I thought I must have misunderstood. Me? I'd never seen Mrs. Crier before, so why would she be here to see me? I'd assumed she was here to see them.

"Me?" I asked.

Mom and Dad both nodded.

Mrs. Crier said something to me, but I didn't get any of it. I didn't have any idea why she was at our house, and I felt very self-conscious. She must have taken this in, because she reached into her leather purse and pulled out a pen and pad. Then she wrote something and handed the pad to me:

I'm glad to meet you, Gustie. Your dad brought me here because I have something to show you.

Now I was even more puzzled.

Dad reached for the pad Mrs. Crier had used and wrote me a message that read:

Do you notice anything . . . well . . . different about Elaine?

Now I felt embarrassed. I *did* notice something different. She was so beautiful. But I was sure Dad hadn't meant that, so I looked her over more carefully.

"No," I said.

As if I'd given just the right answer, they smiled.

"Watch," Mrs. Crier mouthed as she held back the curtain of glossy hair that covered the right side of her head. First, I noticed a pearl earring. Then, with complete surprise, I saw that she was wearing a hearing aid. It was so tiny that it looked like a little button inside her ear.

I drew in my breath. As I was reacting, Mrs. Crier had been writing on the pad:

I'm not exactly old.

We all laughed.

She stayed for dinner, which gave me a chance to notice how well she understood the conversation at the table. She hardly missed a thing. At a point later in the evening, Mrs. Crier demonstrated how little she could hear without the hearing aid. She took it out of her ear, turned her back to us, and had us say things and make little noises at different distances from her. She could hear us only when we were standing very close to her. When she put her hearing aid back in, though, she really heard a lot more. Maybe she didn't hear as well as someone with normal hearing, but the hearing aid made a big difference.

Thanks to Mrs. Crier's visit, I felt good about going to my hearing aid appointment. On the day of my appointment, Mom picked me up right after school. It was the first really cold fall day; my new wool skirt felt like a lucky charm that would make the appointment go well.

Mom drove to a shopping center on the edge of town and parked the car in front of a tan brick building that included a pharmacy and a few offices. A sign above one of the plate glass windows said Midwest Hearing Center. I could make out a waiting room just beyond the glass.

After we went in, a receptionist took our names and asked us to sit down. Mom had to fill out another page of information with our address and insurance coverage.

Mom said something as she completed the form. From her gesture, I could tell it was something like, "Oh, I almost forgot these." She had brought along some charts that showed the results of my hearing tests over the last few months. The one on top had a curved line plummeting from top to bottom that reminded me of half a roller coaster hump.

Mom took the form and the charts to the receptionist while I looked over the waiting room magazines. Before I'd chosen one to leaf through, the receptionist motioned for me to follow her.

"Here goes," I thought.

"I'll be out here," Mom told me, giving me a reassuring smile.

I nodded and gave her sort of a scared smile. I felt less sure of being here now. When I walked past an elderly man being ushered out, my confidence went down another notch. At least he's smiling, I told myself. Then I swallowed the imaginary lump in my throat.

The receptionist said, "Hi, Gustie, I'm Barbara," while also pointing to her name tag.

"Hi", I replied.

We walked down a short hallway, and when we came to the second door to the left, Barbara motioned for me to go inside. "This is our testing room," she told me unnecessarily.

I had seen enough testing rooms in the past three months to recognize one right away. Usually, they looked like little boxes with thick carpeting, soundproof walls, and measurement equipment. This one was no exception.

At the sight of the room, I felt my courage draining away fast. Nobody had told me I'd have to have more tests. Weren't all those charts we'd brought along enough? The most recent one was less than a week old.

I jumped slightly as Barbara touched my arm. She must have said something that I'd completely missed.

"I'm sorry," I told her, "I didn't get what you said." I realized that I'd been staring trancelike at one of the machines.

"There won't be much testing today," she said, reassuring me with her look as much as with her words. "Mr._____[I think she said Hollis] is just going to run a quick one or two." The name of the man hadn't come through very well, but I knew it would probably be on a name tag so I didn't ask Barbara to repeat it. Now that we were in this very quiet, special room, I could hear very well. It wasn't a really rock bottom bad day of hearing, though.

I nodded.

"Why don't you sit down. He'll be here in a minute."

"Okay, Thanks," I told her, and my smile was more genuine this time.

Although I was used to waiting a long time for doctors, Mr. Hollis, the hearing aid counselor, didn't keep me sitting there long.

"Hello, Gustie," the middle-aged man in a loud plaid sport coat said as he walked in. I quickly checked his name tag; his name was *Collins*. He was carrying a large piece of pegboard with different hearing aid models fastened to it. I was relieved to see that most of them were tiny. There was even one that looked like Mrs. Crier's. Still, they looked so artificial; I couldn't imagine wearing one or having it be a part of myself whenever I was awake.

"Hi," I responded.

He was looking over the charts.

"I see that Dr. Gleaves has been very thorough. All I'll need to do today is check to see what your hearing level is now and check you for word discrimination. This information is important in choosing the model that is likely to do the best job in your individual case."

I could hear him so well that understanding him gave me a funny feeling, like, why did I even need a hearing aid? I supposed it was because the little room was totally absent of any distracting background noises. It could also have been because Mr. Collins was sitting no more than two feet away from me and he was careful to look right at me when he spoke. Still, it was a weird feeling.

"Okay," I told him.

For the next fifteen or twenty minutes, I raised my finger in response to various tones that came through.

"Okay," he told me. "We're all done with that."

I smiled at him. It hadn't been so bad.

"Now we'll try out a few of the models you see here on this board," he explained. "I'm going to say some words; you repeat them after me. That will tell me how many words you can hear with each model, which will determine the best hearing aid for you."

"Okay," I said.

He began with one very much like Mrs. Crier's. It looked like a little button. Mr. Collins got up from his chair and walked closer to me so that he could ease the hearing aid into my ear. It felt cold and funny.

He flicked it on and went back to his chair, turning so that I couldn't see his mouth as he said the words.

He said something that was very mushy-sounding.

"I didn't get that one," I told him.

"Carve," he said.

"Carve," I repeated.

"Good," he said.

"Good," I repeated.

Then there was another mushy one.

"_____ire," he said.

There was a sound, very faint and brief, at the start of the word that I didn't hear right. Deciding that it might have been a w, I said, "Wire."

On through the list of words he went, with me getting some of them and not others. Once or twice he came over to me and adjusted the volume of the hearing aid. Then he tried another model and took me through a different word list. Again, I got some of those and not others. The third hearing aid was terrible because everything Mr. Collins said sounded like hissing. The fourth one, the last model he tried on me, was more like the first two, with some words coming through and not others.

Then we were finished and he was looking at me again.

"That does it," he told me. Then he looked down at some notes he'd made and picked up one of the hearing aids. I think it was the second one we'd tried.

Holding it up, he said, "You heard a few more words with this one. I think it's the best model for you."

And that was it, except for an impression of my ear. They poured some cold, gooey stuff into my left ear to make a mold of the canal's shape. Mr. Collins explained that a little piece of plastic the exact shape of the mold would fasten onto my hearing aid and give it a more comfortable fit. It would take about three days for my hearing aid to be ready.

"We'll call you." said Mr. Collins.

Crinkling Thunder

·

The little tan hearing aid was nestled on a bed of velvet in its box. When I looked at the small plastic aid, I felt good. It must surely have the power to make things right again or they wouldn't have given it to me. It would be like a pair of glasses, I decided, or my contact lenses. People who couldn't see right without them could do just fine when wearing them. If ears were like eyes, I'd be a 20/20, or close, once it was in my ear and I got used to it.

"Okay, I guess I'm ready," I told my parents. We were in the living room.

Sort of afraid that I'd break the little instrument, I gingerly lifted it from its box. It didn't weigh much more than a silver dollar. I put the plastic piece shaped like my ear canal into my ear and the little crescent of plastic with the battery and stuff inside just behind my ear. No cord. No box in my bra.

It was ready. All I had to do was turn the switch to *on*.

In the seconds before I did, I thought of all kinds of things—sitting at Jacob's with the old gang from the beach and giggling at a joke, listening to a whispered secret, and hearing the Top 40 along with them. I also thought of going to school and hearing the teachers and students without the dread of wondering if I'd seem like a dunce because I'd missed something important. This little machine was going to make me a part of life again!

"Here I go," I told my parents. Smiling at them, I turned the hearing aid's tiny switch.

But everything went wrong. I heard this terrible, grating screech. I yanked the hearing aid off and put my hand over my ear, which was tingling and itching and hurting from the awful sound.

"What *was* that?" I asked.

Mom and Dad looked stricken. Dad swallowed as if he had a lump in his throat. Mom's eyes suddenly filled up. "It was my voice," she said. "I must have shouted without realizing it. Oh, honey," she said grabbing my hand and giving it a little squeeze, "give it another try. It's going to take all of us time to get used to it."

"It's not your fault, Mom. That wasn't a voice. It was some kind of rock sound." What I didn't say was that I could hear her today, so this experiment really upset me. Mom had a beautiful voice; I didn't want to wear a hearing aid that would steal my memory of her musical voice. Besides, I hadn't even heard any words.

"Take it back," I told them, thrusting the aid into Dad's hand. Then I ran upstairs.

Of course I tried the hearing aid again. Mr. Collins had recommended that I break it in by wearing it no more than an hour a day. Before trying it in school, he suggested that I use it a lot at home.

I tried. I really tried. There's no doubt in my mind that I wanted it to work. After I'd fled into my room after that first try, I'd realized that maybe the machine had accidentally been turned up too high. I couldn't be a quitter. I owed it to myself to try. So I forced myself.

The next time I used it, I left it in my ear for half an hour when nobody else was home. I did hear lots of sounds—Jasmine scratching in her litter box, the refrigerator door closing, and pots and pans rattling as I put them away.

But the human voice just didn't sound right for some reason. Oh, I heard voices, but the words were all fuzzy. I turned on TV and heard a drone that I knew was dialogue, but the words were all mishmashed together.

When I tried wearing it again around my parents, that didn't work either. Although I was very careful to turn the volume switch to its lowest setting with Mom, her voice still sounded terrible. Even with lots and lots of practice, her words just weren't intelligible. Dad's voice was different but not any easier to understand. His was sort of a low rumble that echoed and made my ear itch.

I got very depressed. I began having terrible headaches after wearing the hearing aid for more than a few minutes. In fact, the headaches were so bad and wearing the aid took so much out of me that I missed some school. But I stuck with it and got up to an hour a day with it.

The day came for me to try the aid in school for the first time. I guess from the way things were going at home I should have been prepared for how they would go in school; but, to tell you the truth, I wasn't. I had faith that the hearing aid would work out sooner or later and that one day all that garbling would clear into words I could understand. For some reason, I thought that happy day would occur in school.

Before I go any further, let me tell you that no one could even see the hearing aid. I wore my hair curled softly just short of my shoulders; the curls hid the plastic crescent behind my ear and the little piece that went into my ear canal. It wasn't as if I was trying to hide it, but I was glad it didn't show. I didn't want people to see it, label me handicapped, and maybe pity me. I didn't want to look different than I had when I could still hear.

I was excited about trying the hearing aid for the first time in school. Mom had informed my teachers that I'd be wearing it, so they were kind of prepared. I knew Miss Hartman would be the most understanding of my teachers; that's why I decided to try the aid in her class first. I knew she wouldn't blast me away by shouting or embarrass me by saying something in class like, "Testing 1, 2, 3. Gustie, can you hear me?" She had winked at me in the hall before class, and we'd both crossed our fingers in a gesture of mutual hope that it would help. Her involvement—her caring about what happened with the hearing aid—made me feel more relaxed than I might have been.

I began by turning the hearing aid on very low. I could raise the volume later if I had to. I knew by now that it was more comfortable to start with sound that was on the soft side than sound that blared.

"Please let it work," I implored in a silent little prayer.

When I turned it on, I could hear Miss Hartman talking to the class, but the words all ran together. *"There must be something wrong,"* I thought. But the more I strained to separate the sounds into words, the worse it seemed. I felt like I had a rock inside my stomach. After a few minutes, I just turned the hearing aid off.

Not willing to give up too soon, I decided to give it another try. Later in the period, when my classmates were taking turns translating sentences, I turned the aid back on. I thought that maybe some of their voices would be clearer than others. But, I was wrong. It was awful! I could hear this voice and that voice, but no words.

The worst part, though, was the distracting sounds the other students were making. They didn't even seem to notice them. Jason Clindaniel, who sat directly behind me, was making a really weird noise. While voices droned a Latin translation, I heard a long r-i-i-i-p and crinkling behind me. It was all I could do not to turn around and see what he was doing. Maybe he had torn a page out of a notebook or balled up a piece of paper to throw away. Maybe he was leafing through his notebook or checking a few words in the textbook's glossary. Whatever he was doing drowned out the steady drone of the human voice that made no sense.

A little later, I nearly jumped out of my seat when a horrible, very loud sound blasted its way into my ear. To my amazement, it had only been the girl across from me sneezing. I saw another sneeze coming and quickly switched the hearing aid off.

My head throbbed. Although I left the hearing aid in my ear, I wanted to rip it off and run from the room. I stayed and thought how ironic it was that I got less from class with the hearing aid than on my bad days of hearing when I could hear almost nothing. At least during the quiet days when I couldn't hear, the little crinkles—crinkles like destructive rays bombarding somebody in a sci-fi film—didn't distract me from thinking constructively about a lesson. The quiet at least gave me the chance to read over a lesson or translate to myself in class. But that peace was broken now with the hearing aid because I could be startled by any loud noise. Everything from a chair scraping the floor to knuckles cracking was magnified to a horrible loudness. And of course there was the bad joke of the wordless humming that I knew came through as English to the others.

Finally, seemingly hours later but really only fifty minutes after I'd turned on the hearing aid, class was over. I stayed behind to let Miss Hartman know how it had gone, but I could tell that she'd already noticed my discomfort and already suspected that it'd been a bomb.

As she walked over toward my chair and sat down in one of the student chairs, I reached behind my ear and gently pulled off the hearing aid. Although I didn't feel like being that gentle with it, I did know its cost.

"I feel like tossing it into the wastebasket," I told her as I eyed the metal container near her desk.

"I could tell you were having a bad time of it." She had to repeat this three times before I got it. My hearing was so-so, and the headache wasn't helping things.

"I feel so tired," I told her, "I don't know how I can do any homework now. I just want to go home and go to bed."

"Maybe that's what you should do then, Gustie. Can I help any? I want to, but I'm not sure how to. Did you get anything anybody said while the aid was on?" Again, she had to repeat parts of sentences, but she didn't seem irritated.

"It was a jumble, loud enough but not clear at all, Miss Hartman," I confided. "But the papers crinkling and knuckles popping were really loud."

"Well, about all anybody can do in life, Gustie, is to give something a good, fair try. Give the hearing aid a fair trial, and hope that it will help. If it doesn't, keep in mind that there are surely other doors open to you. Your ultimate happiness doesn't depend just on how well you use a hearing aid."

"Sort of like it's better to try and fail than never to try at all?" I asked.

She smiled at me and nodded. "Yes, but remember that if you fail at any one thing, it doesn't mean you'll necessarily fail at another. You can't will yourself to hear normally again, but you should give yourself a chance to hear with the hearing aid."

She had to repeat this several times before I understood her. "Maybe I expected too much from it."

"Maybe so, but there's nothing wrong with going into something with a positive attitude. Okay?"

"Okay."

I tried the hearing aid three more times in school in different classes, but I had the same results as I did that first time. I heard the crinkles and not the important things. I had terrible headaches. I slept a lot, sometimes sixteen hours a day, and my grades went down because most nights I was too tired to study.

Finally, Mom and Dad realized that the hearing aid wasn't helping me any. They had a phone conference with Dr. Gleaves in Chicago and then decided that I shouldn't wear it again.

It wasn't my last try with a hearing aid, though. Dr. Gleaves had decided I should try a slightly different model. It was shaped differently, but when I tried it, I got the same results.

The day before Thanksgiving, Mom was flitting around the house like a little bird, tidying and getting ready for the dinner we were having the next day. Dad's two sisters and their families, which included four little kids, would be with us, and we'd be having a traditional turkey dinner with all the trimmings.

"Have you tried the hearing aid today?" Mom asked out of the blue as she pushed a broom around the kitchen before washing the floor.

It seemed like a funny time to bring up the subject. "Mom, I think I've given it a fair trial. It doesn't make the useful sounds louder or clearer, and I'm tired of all the headaches. I think I'm just going to have to get ready to be a deaf per . . ."

"Don't say that Gustie. I'm sure we'll find something to save your hearing." The look of panic in her eyes stunned me.

Wasn't she aware that my good days were getting fewer and fewer? *Save my hearing, save my hearing,* seemed to be everybody's song. Yeah, and what if we couldn't?

"Tomorrow's a holiday," I reminded her. "Let's just drop it and enjoy the company."

"Actually, I think you should wear the aid when the company is here. Maybe with a good range of voices, you'll discover that some of them come through very well."

I couldn't believe she was saying that. I'd told Mom and Dad in detail about the jumble in school. Hadn't they listened to me at all?

Then I had an inspiration. "Okay, Mom. I'll wear it for the dinner, but only if you'll promise me now that if it doesn't work, we're through with it."

She thought it over for a full minute and then nodded, saying, "That seems fair enough, but you'll try, won't you? Don't decide beforehand what will or won't work."

Boy, did that make me mad. I was the one with all the positive thoughts about the hearing aid. I had been actually enthusiastic about it and had counted on its working, not aggravating me to extremes as it had.

To keep the peace, I told her, "Yes."

And I did try, but the end result was only a giant headache that finally ruined all my pleasure in a holiday I normally liked. I'd always liked my two aunts and their families, especially the little kids. But this Thanksgiving they did not seem like the people I knew and loved.

They were obstacles. They were noise. They were Aunt Marty cackling. They were Uncle Jim's hacking cough as he chain smoked. They were Aunt Gloria shouting at me even though Mom and I told her that wouldn't help. They were four kids screaming, especially the little girls, who squealed in delight at the slightest provocation.

The hearing aid just magnified some sounds into distracting noise and yet managed not to let me understand conversation. I only heard a drone spiked by squealing, coughing, and cackling. The noise was so loud it made me wince. Even when I turned the hearing aid down to its lowest setting, the sound still grated on my nerves. I felt confused and alone.

I escaped to my bedroom shortly after dinner. "Thanksgiving was a bomb, Jasmine," I told my cat, who had wisely hidden in my room all afternoon from the grabby eighteen-month-old baby.

Jasmine rubbed against me.

Just before I crawled into bed, I took the hearing aid out of my pocket, placed it in its box, and said, *"Arrivederci,* hearing aid."

Silent Nights . . . And Days

·

For the next couple of months, I took life one day at a time. My hearing was bad more than it was good, and each time it improved a little, it wasn't as good as it had been the time before.

My whole life revolved around my hearing. It even affected family customs.

I guess all families have their traditions, and digging into "The Box" around the first of December was one of ours. The Box was crammed full of special Christmas decorations. There were candles, the velvet wreath Aunt Marty had made, felt stockings, and the other things we so carefully repacked after each Christmas.

"Here's my stocking," I announced ceremoniously to Mom and Dad as I pulled away the tissue paper to reveal the bright red stocking. It had my name on it in green felt and a Frosty the Snowman look-alike Gram had sewn on it. Mom and Dad, who smiled at their first glimpse of my stocking, each also had a custom Gram-made stocking.

While Mom unwrapped her favorite Christmas candle, whose sides looked like stained glass church windows when the candle was burning, she said something I didn't get.

"What?"

"It's held up well," she repeated for my benefit. Then she cast a smile Dad's way and said what she had said every single Christmas that I could remember, "Dad gave it to me the first Christmas we were married."

He was over by the stereo slipping a record out of an album with Bing Crosby's picture on it. I didn't get what he had said, but the conversation about the candle was such a ritual in our household that I knew anyway.

"I promised her I'd take her to see Chartres Cathedral someday," he said. Then he winked and put the record on the turntable.

All of a sudden, this awful noise made me tighten my fingers around the stocking I'd just lifted from The Box.

In a tinny sort of way, the melody of "White Christmas" came through, but the voice was a joke. Bing Crosby had turned into Donald Duck with a cold. It was so horrible a discovery that I wanted to tear the record off the turntable and shatter it into a hundred pieces. I loved "White Christmas"—it was a beautiful song—but what I was hearing this year wasn't even music. It seemed too cruel.

I watched Mom put the Chartres candle on a bookshelf and Dad read the album cover. They looked so normal, like they had all the other Christmases I could remember. But I felt so different, I might just as well have dropped in from Mars.

Dad waved the cover at me to get my attention and said something that I didn't understand. This was, by the way, supposedly one of my good days of hearing. It's just that "good" wasn't very good anymore.

"Is it still your favorite?" he repeated.

What could I say?

"I . . . it sounds . . . different," I stammered.

Dad, I guess thinking it was too soft for me to hear, turned the volume up. Criminy! It could have been the theme song for a horror movie. It certainly wasn't good old reliable Bing and my favorite Christmas song.

"Turn it down, please," I ordered.

"Huh?"

Instead of being nice, I walked over to Dad and let my eyes bore into him. I was really upset about the way the record sounded, but I also felt hurt because Dad seemed to think that a simple little volume increase would do the trick. After all the trouble with the hearing aids making a blaring jumble of meaningless sound, how could Dad think that would magically solve anything?

"*Turn it down*," I ordered again, not using much or any voice. Only my heart was shouting.

The magic of The Box was spoiled. Flinging the stocking that I was still holding onto the dining room table, I ran to my bedroom and slammed the door.

Jasmine was curled up on my bed. I ran to her and buried my head into her softness as tears started inching down my cheeks in wide, burning rivers.

"*I hate Dad*," I thought. How could he stick his head in the sand like an ostrich?

The weird, zithered melody and Donald Duck voice went through my mind. Would I ever be able to remember the way "White Christmas" really sounded, or would this stupid version be the way I thought of the song for the rest of my life?

"And I'm only fifteen!" I told Jasmine, who had begun to wash herself. I wished I were a cat.

There was a knock on my door. Jasmine had heard it too and had looked up momentarily from her bath.

Brushing away my tears as well as I could, I called, "Come in." Then I propped myself into a sitting position with my back against the bed's headboard. Jasmine was washing herself again.

Mom walked in.

"What happened downstairs?" she asked as she sat down on a corner of my bed.

I realized that I was finding out as each day went by what it means not to hear right. Maybe I should have known that The Box would be different this year, but I'd gotten pleasantly lost in its fun and forgotten to be ready for some additional sign that nothing was the same.

I said, "The Box was like always. You know, with our stockings and your Chartres candle. And then Dad put the record on . . . "

And boom! Everything changed. No visions of sugarplums. No Christmas peace. No letting the music bring back memories or make a happy background for holiday decorating.

"And?"

"I could hear it, Mom, but it sounded so awful. It sounded like some people had deliberately recorded a sick version of 'White Christmas.'" I knew my words didn't describe the way it had sounded, and it was hard to believe that only I had heard the screwed-up version.

Mom seemed to be waiting for more.

"And then Dad turned it up . . . "

"It made it even worse?" Mom supplied the rest for me when I let the sentence trail off.

I nodded.

Her look of understanding—a certain gentleness that seemed to glow in her eyes—made me feel a little better, but then she ruined it by telling me to think positively. As if that would turn Donald Duck back into Bing Crosby.

Why couldn't they understand?

One of the aftereffects of meningitis was that I got tired very easily. Trying to cope with the big changes in my life also wore me out. Suddenly, it was a big deal to do anything.

In January, right after our winter break, I decided to take Miss Hartman up on her offer to grade me only on written work. Maybe that sounds like an easy decision to make, but it was awfully hard for me. It made me different from the rest of the class. As Miss Hartman had promised, I didn't get easy work. In fact, she had me translating work much harder than the stuff in the regular textbook. But the rest of the class didn't realize that, and I worried about what they might be saying and thinking about me. Maybe they thought I had it easy.

I also decided to forget French. A part of me wanted to stay in the class. Deep inside, I knew I could do the work, given a chance by a teacher as supportive as Miss Hartman. Mr. Armour's note still turned me off, though, and I had enough problems without him adding more. Instinct warned me that unless he really wanted me in his class, I'd either flunk French or just barely pass. I just couldn't do oral work like I used to, and Mr. Armour was big on spelling bees in French and stuff like that.

I dropped French and concentrated on my three other classes: Latin, English, and American history. I would wait until next semester to add math and any others.

In school, my other two teachers were nice to me, but they were not as helpful as Miss Hartman was. Mrs. Zenor still had the habit of shouting at me. I'd understood her pretty well for a while, especially right after I returned to school, but my changing hearing now interfered with that.

On my better hearing days, Mrs. Zenor's shouting sounded like a jumble of noises, not like words. On the bad days—which most of them were now—I felt like I was watching a weird, meaningless pantomime. I'm sure she thought she was helping, and when people tried so hard, I wanted very much to please them. I felt apologetic and disappointed in myself when I couldn't. I never talked to Mrs. Zenor about it because I still wasn't sure of myself and where I fit in. Sometimes I pretended that I didn't know the answer to her oral question, when the truth was that I didn't know what she'd asked me.

She also showed her concern by asking me at least once a week if I'd had any good news from the doctors about my hearing. The first couple of times she asked this, I felt good. Later on, it started upsetting me. She seemed like one more person waiting for a miracle. What, I wondered, would my life be like if the miracle didn't happen? That question really scared me. I worried that I might be just one big disappointment to everybody if my hearing didn't get better.

Mr. Railsback, my American history teacher, sort of ignored me. He didn't try to talk to me, and he didn't call on me in class.

I wasn't getting nearly as much out of class discussions as I used to, but I felt proud for going to school and keeping up with assignments. I read the textbooks more carefully than I ever had when I could hear normally, and I also read extra books from the library.

Mom and Dad, of course, could tell that the days of good hearing were becoming fewer and farther between. I was still going to Chicago every Tuesday either to see Dr. Gleaves or to the hospital for tests that his staff couldn't give me at his office. I didn't have to check into the hospital and stay. They just did a test or two and sent me home the same day. I think I must have had every hearing test there is, plus more complicated tests like brain scans.

Mom and Dad even took me to a famous clinic in Minnesota. I didn't see how testing my digestive tract and just about everything else would help my hearing, but I tried to be nice about it the five days we were there. It wasn't easy. I was very scared. For one thing, most of the doctors treated me like a body without feelings. Although Mom and Dad were supportive, they didn't tell me much. It occurred to me then, for the first time, that maybe they didn't know much to tell.

The best thing to come out of all the tests was that one of the doctors suggested I take speechreading lessons. I had never heard of speechreading. The doctor told me that it was a more modern term for *lipreading*. Lipreading isn't really accurate because you have to do much more than read somebody's lips. A lot of people, including my parents, say lipreading when they mean speechreading.

After we got home from Minnesota, Mom and Dad found a speechreading class for me. It was really interesting; I learned things I had never even thought about before. For example, there are sounds that are made exactly the same way, so the only way to tell them apart is to hear them. Try saying *mat, bat,* and *pat.* Watch and feel how you make the first sound of each word. Well, if you aren't deaf, you can hear the difference when the words are spoken out loud, but the three sounds look exactly alike on the lips and they can easily stump a speechreader trying to follow a conversation. In speechreading class I learned to watch for these stumbling blocks. If I thought someone said "Hand me the patches," and there were no patches around, my mind knew to quickly substitute a *b* or an *m* for the *p* in *patches*: "Hand me the matches," usually made much more sense.

This isn't to say that speechreading solved all my problems. Far from it! It wasn't the same as hearing. For one thing, there are lots of pitfalls in speechreading. Speakers with thin lips, broken teeth, or mustaches make it awfully hard. People who talk very fast or do not look directly at the speechreader do, too. It's especially hard to read names, and when the topic of conversation suddenly changes or when there are lots of speakers, it's hard to follow what's going on. I also have found that my success depends a lot upon how I feel. If I am tired or have a headache or something on my mind, it messes up my concentration, so I miss some of the visual clues I need in order to speechread well.

It was a good thing that I had those lessons and knew the basics of speechreading. My hearing was getting worse everyday. It finally got so that I couldn't hear anything at all.

Dogs barked silently. There were no car horn honks. Thunder was something I felt in my chest but did not hear. People's lips moved, but no matter how much they shouted, there was no sound at all.

In mid-January, I had a string of totally silent days. I kept waiting for my hearing to bounce back up. Every morning when I woke up, I said something out loud in my bedroom, hoping as hard as I'd ever hoped for anything that I'd hear at least a tiny sound.

What would it mean if my hearing never came back?

I thought of robins singing in May, the sound of rain, a knock on the door. I thought of people cheering for the home team, the ping of an elevator bell, and the crunch when someone bites into an apple. I even thought of sounds I didn't like—sounds that were useful because they warned people of things like tornadoes, trains rushing down the tracks, and ambulances or fire trucks.

If I ever had a husband, would I hear his voice? Would I hear my kids say their first words and call me mommy?

Would I ever go to church and be able to hear the sermon?

Would I be able to sing happy birthday to my family and friends on key? What would my life be like if I never heard Christmas carols normally again? How would I know the changes in the Top 40? Would my favorite classical music be only a memory for the rest of my life? Would I wake up one morning and realize that I'd forgotten it all, lost music?

I just didn't know.

I even got out the hearing aid that Mom and Dad still hadn't returned and tried it once more. I turned the volume up all the way, and then put the TV on full blast, but I heard absolutely nothing. Thinking that the hearing aid might need a fresh battery, I replaced the one that had been inside, but it didn't make any difference. There was no sound.

Remembering how loud the hearing aid had made crinkling paper sound, I tried balling up a sheet of typing paper right next to the ear with the hearing aid in it. No crinkle. No nothing.

Still wearing the hearing aid, I went through the house in a frenzy, banging things, dropping things, clapping my hands—nothing. Not one sound.

The silence was so scary that one day when I was home alone, I screamed as loudly as I could. I thought I'd go crazy if I didn't hear something—anything! But when I couldn't even hear my own screech, I felt sort of unreal, like I was in a nightmare I couldn't wake up from.

On a Tuesday during this string of bad days, Mom and I went to Chicago to see Dr. Gleaves. Dad had a patient about ready to have her baby, so he couldn't go.

As we were getting ready to leave, Mom said, "Wish us luck, Gordon." I wondered if her voice sounded scared. The speechreading lessons had encouraged me to watch body language, and it looked to me like Mom was in need of reassurance. Her smile didn't quite reach her eyes.

The worry wrinkle between Dad's eyebrows was deep that day, almost like a scar, but he tried to hide whatever he was feeling.

He said something to Mom. Then he turned to me. When he briefly put his hand under my chin and chucked it, I figured out that probably he was telling me to keep my chin up.

"I'll try," I told him as I gave him a peck on the cheek.

I could tell that he really wanted to go to Chicago with us, but Mom and I both understood that he couldn't desert a patient ready to have her baby. As an obstetrician's daughter, I was used to babies arriving during our family get-togethers, on holidays, and in the middle of the night. Dad never complained.

He walked around to the other side of the car and kissed Mom, and as he waved us off, he mouthed, "Have a safe trip."

Since Mom had to watch her driving, we said little on the way there. I made my mind almost blank and just watched the dreary winter countryside, the steel mills, and the oil refineries as we sped along the road.

I thought I'd be having another test of some kind, but Mrs. Blumenthal, the nurse, led us to a room I'd never been in before. Apparently, it was the doctor's private office—his inner sanctum, as Dad called his own consultation room. This one was all red-leathery and smelled like Pledge. They probably used a whole can just to shine the biggest desk I've ever seen. It's gleaming wood rose up out of a sea-colored carpet like a ship.

Dr. Gleaves looked like a president or something behind the desk. He greeted us very formally, Not knowing what else to do, I said hi and smiled at him. He smiled back and motioned for us to sit in the two leather chairs facing his desk.

He didn't say much to me. He talked to Mom like I wasn't really there, although by this time I expected that. It still made me feel pretty cruddy, though. I might have been able to follow most of the conversation, but he kept a pipe clenched between his teeth as he spoke. Pipes are another speechreading pitfall.

Looking uncomfortable, Dr. Gleaves finally took the pipe out of his mouth. I almost wished he hadn't because the one sentence I read perfectly was, "Frankly, Mrs. Blaine, we've done all for your daughter that is medically possible."

Mom looked like somebody had just shot her in the heart with an arrow.

"Are you sure?" she asked in what I imagined was a very soft voice.

Dr. Gleaves nodded sympathetically.

I wanted to hold Mom and comfort her. I knew she was hurting, and her expression frightened me. Getting in the way of my wanting to comfort her was my need to beg her not to hang onto hopes and dreams, not to chase rainbows for a pot of gold that probably would always be out of reach.

"*Love the real me*," I wanted to plead. "*Love the deaf me, Mama*."

I didn't pay attention to much else while we were in the doctor's office. I was thinking that the way this worked out didn't really surprise me. In a way, I guess I had expected it. Although no one had told me that my hearing might leave completely and forever, it wasn't that hard to figure it out. It had been going down, down, until finally it left completely.

Moving almost as if in a dream, Mom and I left the doctor's inner sanctum. In the elevator on our way down to the parking garage, Mom was struggling not to cry. The only thing that mattered to me right then wasn't how I'd learn to be a deaf person or what my future might be like, but Mom. I ached for her.

"Mom," I said, reaching out for her hand, "I know what Dr. Gleaves said. Please believe me, everything will work out. I love you so much."

We hugged each other as the elevator went down.

Nothing in Common

·

If I hadn't liked Miss Hartman so well, I wouldn't have agreed to see
Mr. Tate. He was one of the special education teachers at my school.

"_____ like _____ Gustie _____ school easier," Miss
Hartman told me. The parts I couldn't speechread might as well have
been "and blah, blah, blah." Just a few months ago I had heard her so
well. Now I wanted to reach over and flick an imaginary switch to turn
her voice back on.

At first, I caught myself nodding as if I'd understood every word,
but knowing that she wanted to help me encouraged me to level with
her.

"I'm sorry," I admitted, "for some reason, I didn't get what you
said." It was weird how I could read some people's lips so well and not
others'. Unfortunately, Miss Hartman was one of the "others."

"_____," she said.

Oh brother. This time not a thing came through. Then I realized
why. Miss Hartman barely moved her upper lip as she spoke, and that
greatly reduced the visual clues I needed to understand her. Somehow,
pinning down a reason for the difficulty made me feel better about it.

Pointing to my notebook, she mouthed, I think, "May I?" When I
nodded, she opened the notebook, pulled a pen out of her pocket, and
began writing. The note read:

> You don't have to apologize, Gustie. I just said that I think
> you'll like Mr. Tate. He's one of those easy-to-talk-to people. I

have a hunch that he knows a few ways to make school easier for you. You've done a good job on your own, but I think you could use a little extra help.

She was right. It was only February, but I could see a big difference from when I'd come back to school in October. I thought of the "holes" in my notes and missed points of class discussion that popped up later on tests. It was crummy to have to take a lower grade just because I'd never heard part of a class discussion. I remembered teachers like Mr. Armour who seemed to think of me one year as Miss Industrious and the next as Instant Freak, and I thought of friends who had faded away. "Okay, I'll go," I finally said.

Even though I'd agreed to it, that didn't mean I felt good about going to Mr. Tate's office. I can't really explain why I dreaded it, except that going seemed like I might be losing the old me. Even though I realized that I was probably going to be deaf for the rest of my life, I wanted to hang onto the way life was.

I was going mainly because I liked Miss Hartman too much to be "difficult."

I didn't know what Mr. Tate would be like. I pictured him as the fatherly type, with silvering hair. He'd probably be wearing a cardigan sweater—the kind that buttons partway up and leaves some shirt and a tie showing—to cover a potbelly.

Because I didn't really want to go, the walk upstairs to his office seemed to take too little time. The door to room 211 was open, I noticed as my heartbeat speeded up. I had counted on a few extra seconds to get myself together before knocking on a closed door, stalling, as I usually did, before walking into my dentist's office.

Just as I took a deep breath, he looked up and saw me.

"You must be Gustie," the man grading papers at his desk said as I approached his doorway. "Come on in."

My first impression of him was that he didn't look anything like I thought he would. He was probably in his mid-twenties, with sandy hair and lively eyes. He also had a warm smile that melted some of my resistance.

"Mr. Tate?"

Nodding in answer to my question, he said, "Pull up a chair and sit down." I noticed that his lips were easy to read.

For some reason I wasn't sure of, I felt stubborn. I was going to keep standing and make it a very short visit. Then his clear gray eyes seemed to ask me to help him out. I sat.

Instead of staying in the chair behind the bulky desk, he got up and pulled over a chair that matched mine and sat down. *"Chalk one up for Mr. Tate,"* I thought. I also noticed that he was wearing brown cords and a long-sleeved plaid shirt rolled up at the sleeves. No cardigan. No flab.

"I take it you aren't overjoyed to be here."

I had the funny feeling that he was looking into me just as a person looks through a window to see what's inside. "That's right," I told him. "But it's nothing personal," I quickly added. I wasn't trying to be rude. It just didn't feel right to be talking to a special education teacher. Special education was for handicapped kids.

"Want to tell me about it?" he offered.

Our eyes met and he smiled. To my amazement, I found that I really did want to talk about it. The trouble was I didn't know where to begin. How could I ever describe how my life had changed? There was so much to tell.

Almost before I knew what was happening, I blurted out, "Nobody's going to make me learn sign language!"

He didn't look as surprised as I felt. Why, of all the stupid things, had I said that? I felt my cheeks burning.

"You're right about that. Nobody is. It's something you've got to want to do. And you don't, I take it. Why?"

The funny thing is that I didn't know why. I had tried to push the idea of sign language way into the back of my mind. Maybe because I connected it with being mute and Mr. Armour's "impoverished life," the idea of learning it scared me.

But what I said was, "I don't need it, Mr. Tate. I can speechread."

I felt pleased with myself. I knew that I was proving to him that I could speechread very well. Mr. Tate's lips were easy to read as long as I watched him closely.

"Yes, you can, Gustie. You can speechread very well—better, in fact, than most deaf people. You have every right to be proud of that."

"Well . . ."

"Let me finish. First of all, you don't have to pretend with me, Gustie. We both know that speechreading is only a substitute for hearing speech. So, in fact, is sign language. I'm not even saying that you should learn to sign.

"A fact of life is that speech—oral communication—is the way most people on our big blue marble communicate. Notice that I said *communicate*. That's the key word. If we communicate, does it really matter how we do it? Is one form of communication inferior to another? Can we really be fair to ourselves if we don't examine all the options and foster techniques that will aid communication? Can we just write off a form of communication that might make life better and easier?"

His gray eyes bored into me, but he didn't look mad at me. I knew he really believed in what he was saying and that he was just trying to help.

"I don't know what to say, Mr. Tate. It sounds okay to sign, but . . . . *But, gee, Mr. Tate, not for me. Not for me.*"

I didn't realize that I was staring at my shoe until I felt him touch my sleeve to get my attention.

"Are you afraid to learn sign language and to meet other hearing-impaired people?" he asked. I imagined that he said this very softly. There was something gentle in his expression.

To my embarrassment, I started to cry. He handed me his big white handkerchief. I didn't think men under forty carried them anymore. I hoped my mascara was as tearproof as the ad said, or else the white cloth would be stained.

He let me cry. Something in his not pushing me to answer right away made me want to answer. Or try to.

"Yes," I admitted when I'd gotten the tears under control. "Yes, I am afraid. But I don't even know why."

"It's okay to be afraid, Gustie, really it is. You are undergoing an enormous change in your life. I think I may even know why you feel afraid. I'd like you to think about it and let me know in a few days what you come up with. Will you do that?"

I nodded. Then we both stood, signaling an end to the brief but emotional meeting.

I knew I wouldn't be back, but I fibbed and said, "Okay, I'll do that, Mr. Tate."

"Please come back soon, even if you don't come up with an answer right away. I'm here every afternoon between three and four o'clock."

"Thanks for talking to me," I told him. then I left, still holding his mascara-stained handkerchief.

That night in bed, I realized that what I wanted more than anything else in the world was to belong. To belong didn't mean to learn sign language. To belong was to be like I used to be. It was to laugh at the burger place with Sara, Dana, and the gang. To belong was cheerleading practice and piano lessons, not trips to see doctors and Say the Word tests. It was being able to talk on the phone, and it was knowing what the actors were saying in a movie and being able to talk about the movie later with friends. It was coming home and not seeing the tension on my parents' faces. It was being able to understand conversations and having the freedom to keep and throw out whatever I wanted to, like everybody else.

To belong was to be normal.

To learn sign language would be to give in to being different. I would never belong then. And not belonging was what scared me more than anything else. I didn't want to be different.

Was I expecting too much from hearing people? Maybe I needed to tell Mrs. Zenor that shouting didn't help. Maybe I should try harder to talk to Mom and Dad. Maybe I also needed to make the first moves with friends and not wait around for them to come to me. Was my isolation my own fault? Since they weren't deaf and couldn't know what it was like, maybe it was up to me to tell them what a big change it made.

When Sara suddenly came to mind, I decided to have a heart-to-heart talk with her over the weekend. Surely we didn't have to throw away our friendship. Maybe she just needed to know that I was still me.

As I lay in bed, I thought of all the things I was going to say to Sara. I'm not sure, but I think I fell asleep with a smile on my face.

Saturday morning I came into the kitchen feeling better than I had for months.

"My," Mom said as she had another cup of coffee while I ate a bowl of Cheerios, "you look happy today."

"I am, Mom. I've decided to go to Sara's and talk to her, heart-to-heart. I've missed her so much."

"I know," Mom said, smiling at me. I'd seen too few smiles like that on her face over the past few months, and it made me feel good.

We stopped talking as I munched. I ate the last spoonful of cereal and said, "You know how you always say to think positive?"

Mom nodded.

"I decided to do that with Sara and also to be the one to make the next move. She can't know what I'm going through unless I explain it to her. I need to know how she feels, too."

"I think a talk with her is a marvelous idea."

I got dressed shortly after that and walked to her house.

Sara answered the door when I knocked. She looked surprised to see me.

"Sara," I said more boldly than I felt, "could I come in for a minute and talk to you?"

She was wearing an old sweatshirt, the one that had been through so many of our painting projects. There were yellow drips from the time we painted an old wooden chest that was now in Sara's room; candied violet stains from the time we helped Dad paint my room; a green handprint from the time we were painting stage scenery in junior high—I had put out my paint-smeared hand to keep Sara from falling backwards after she had stepped on a hammer.

Did she remember all those and other shared times? Did they still mean something to her? Didn't they make her feel as good as they did me? Even as I stood there, I wondered what had happened to us. Maybe it didn't matter as long as we could be close again.

But Sara looked . . . well . . . not warm and friendly, and I felt some of my boldness crumble.

"_____ dash soon, Gustie," she told me. "What do you want?" Her lips weren't too hard to read.

She stood in the doorway as though blocking my entrance to the kitchen where we had baked cookies, made countless cups of hot chocolate, and played Julia Child with whatever food we thought our moms would forgive us for using. The difference between then and now hurt. I hoped she didn't feel as cool as she looked. "*Be positive*," I reminded myself.

"What's happened to us, Sara? To our friendship? Let's talk about it. That's why I'm here."

"We were just kids," she said. "Everything _____ _____, Gustie."

As much as I hated to ask people to repeat things, I really wanted to know everything Sara said today.

"Everything what?" I asked.

She mumbled the word again, but just when I'd filled in the blank with the most likely word on my own, she said, "Changes! Changes! Changes!"

Her impatience struck me like a slap.

She stopped speaking and looked down at her hands. I hoped she might be realizing that, yes, things change, but friendship can grow and change along with life. I was going to tell her this, sure that she'd understand, but she started talking again. I couldn't believe she said what she did.

She raised her eyes from her hands, looked into my eyes, and then she stared at something over my shoulder as she said, "We just don't have anything in common now that you are deaf."

Nothing in common! How could she stand there and say that? What could I say to make her understand? Did she have any idea how much she was hurting me? Was I nobody now that I was deaf?

I felt like either crying or saying something crummy to hurt her back, but the words just wouldn't come out. My voice was paralyzed by the shock of what she'd said.

Nothing in common! How could I put my feelings into words? I felt so empty. It was a little like the Sara I knew and loved had died. It was the death of a friendship. Friendship, after all, takes two people. I felt rejected, confused, and alone. I needed to keep some pride, though; I didn't want Sara to see my tears.

So much for heart-to-heart talks. Trying to control my quivering chin, I looked at Sara and said, "You say we don't have anything in common. Just look at your sweatshirt."

Then I walked away. I had to or I would have broken down.

I really felt sorry for myself all that day, and I cried buckets of tears. Mom didn't help any. She knew, as mothers do, that something was wrong. More wrong than usual, that is. When had anything been right lately? Anyway, she came into my room carrying a tray with cheese, crackers, and some grapes on it. I hadn't eaten lunch.

"I thought you might be ready for a snack," she told me. When I didn't say anything right away, Mom put the tray on the dresser and sat on the edge of my bed. "The visit didn't go well, I take it. I'm so sorry."

I shook my head and said, "Mom, I just don't understand. I've known Sara for so long. We were so close, almost like sisters."

"What happened?" Mom asked, gently pushing my hair away from my eyes.

"Oh, Mom, she, she . . ." I finally choked back my tears and got better control of my voice. "She said we don't have anything in common because I'm deaf now."

Mom held me just like she did when I was a little girl, and I cried. I felt very close to Mom just then.

Later that day, though, I got awfully mad at her. I was nibbling a piece of cheese and looking out my bedroom window at nothing special when I saw Mrs. Marler, Sara's mother, heading for our back door. I crept partway down the stairs and spied on Sara's mother and mine. I just knew they were going to talk about Sara and me.

"*I shouldn't have told Mom*," I thought.

From the place where I was hiding on the stairs, I could see into the kitchen, but I couldn't read their lips because they were too far away. Mom poured Mrs. Marler a cup of coffee. Mrs. Marler looked curious but not mad. Mom, on the other hand, looked ready to spit nails. I wondered if she had phoned Sara's mother and strongly suggested that she come over.

Almost before I knew what was happening, Mom was shaking her forefinger at Sara's mother while Mrs. Marler stood with her hands on her hips in a how-dare-you pose. I could almost see the words being angrily tossed back and forth.

I felt awful. I liked Sara's mother. She and Mom had been friends for years.

About a half hour later Mrs. Marler stormed out and slammed the door. Mom, sitting at the table, sort of crumpled. She had her head in her hands and was crying every bit as hard as I had. I should have gone to her, but I was feeling too sorry for myself. I realized that I blamed Mom and Dad for some of my mixed-up feelings.

Back in my room, I said to Jasmine, "All I do is cause trouble. Nobody is the same because *I'm* not the same. I want to belong in this family. I want to belong at school. I want to belong in friendships. Oh, Jas, you're the only one that's acting the same."

It wasn't until later that I thought of a way I might belong.

A Way To Belong

·

I put my Belonging Plan into effect the first day of school after spring vacation.

Tony Riach, who is two years older than I am, was the unknowing accomplice in my plan. I started doing a few things with Tony after he tutored me in geometry last spring. Geometry, to put it mildly, was not my subject, but Tony was a born teacher and he had me doing pretty well at it. Not only is Tony smart and cute, with dreamy brown eyes, but he is also nice. Ordinarily, Mom and Dad might not have let me date a guy two years older, but even they liked Tony.

Last spring, we saw a few movies together and had a picnic or two. I thought of Tony more as a pal than a boyfriend, if you know what I mean. Tony, unfortunately, had other ideas. He wanted to be lots more serious than I'd ever been with a guy. Although it was hard to admit it to him, I very honestly told him I wasn't ready for that kind of friendship.

He seemed to understand, but he told me to let him know if I ever changed my mind.

I was sure I never would. Only, now my Belonging Plan was going to include Tony.

At school that Monday, I casually—although my knees were knocking together because I was so nervous—dropped a folded piece of notebook paper onto the library table where Tony usually sat during sixth period and right after school. All it said was, I've changed my mind.

I was worried that he'd never answer my note. I had no way of knowing if he still liked me. I hadn't seen much of him since I'd been sick, either, and I didn't know how he would feel about going out with a deaf person.

But Tony came through. A few minutes later, he walked over to the library table where I was pretending to be engrossed in my Latin book.

His note read:

Glad to hear it. How about a ride to Ripton on Saturday to get some maple sugar candy? Pick you up around 1:00?

He waited while I read the note. I was thrilled that he remembered my passion for maple candy. I gave him a nod, sealing our date for Saturday.

The rest of the week didn't go so well. Sara pretty much ignored me. After that morning at her house when she told me we didn't have anything in common anymore, we acted like strangers. We usually only saw each other in Mrs. Zenor's English class. I was still both angry and hurt. So hurt, in fact, that I didn't even want to try to make up because I was afraid she'd just reject me again. Anyway, she was the one who owed me the apology, I kept reminding myself.

Since Sara seemed to be with Marcia Trent a lot, Cindy and Dana had paired off. Our old quartet had broken apart, and I didn't seem to fit in anywhere.

I also had some trouble in American history class that week. I took a test I thought I was more than ready for and found three or four questions that I knew hadn't been in the textbook. Mr. Railsback had apparently padded the book's information by adding a few extras. He was murder to speechread because he wore a full beard and mustache. His facial hair kept me from seeing much of his mouth. And yet for that very reason, I studied extra hard in history. It was disappointing to end up with a *B* instead of an *A* just because I hadn't heard a few comments.

Finally, Saturday came. Mom had liked Tony last spring and seemed glad that I was going out with him. She didn't know that I'd asked him out, but I certainly wasn't going to explain my Belonging Plan to her.

Anyway, I was ready at 1:00, wearing a sweatshirt and jeans. Tony was dressed almost the same.

It was a beautiful sunny day that seemed more like May than March. I felt nervous about my Belonging Plan and tried to keep from twisting my amethyst ring around and around my finger as we rode to Ripton, but it went around lots of times anyway. I missed the kind of small talk most people on dates make as they ride in a car, and I kept wondering what he was thinking.

I could feel the car radio playing. It seemed from the vibrations to be pretty loud, but of course I still couldn't hear it. I never knew for sure how much to raise my voice in order to be heard. I remembered how Mrs. Raymond, our neighbor who wore a hearing aid, used to shout all the time. Not wanting to shout, old person style, I usually talked in a "living room" voice. Lots of people just didn't hear me if other sounds, like people talking in a restaurant or a radio playing, drowned out my voice.

This happened with Tony on our ride. I said something about the car, but he didn't hear me. I didn't repeat it because I figured he couldn't look at the road and me long enough for me to read his lips without taking a terrible chance. Maybe Tony sensed that we couldn't talk easily as we rode because he didn't try to talk to me. He glanced at me now and then, smiled, and held my hand part of the way.

Near Ripton, we stopped at a little country store by an apple orchard. It specialized in cider, homemade candies, and other good things. Tony had taken me there for a celebration after I got my first decent geometry test score. This time, he bought some maple sugar candy shaped like tiny maple leaves for me and some homemade fudge with nuts for himself.

Back inside the car, we rode until we came to some woods along a country road. We got out and hiked into the trees. When we reached a small clearing, Tony spread out a blanket and we sat down and ate some of our candy.

Finally, we started to talk.

"Did you mean it when you said you've changed your mind?" he asked.

He had to repeat this sentence three times. My palms felt damp because I was nervous about my Belonging Plan. I was also embarrassed by my dumb inability to read his lips well. His lips were thin, and he barely moved the upper one when he spoke, but I always felt like there was something wrong with me when I couldn't understand a person.

"Yes," I answered. "I've . . . I've . . . well . . . changed, Tony." All this had sounded fine when I'd rehearsed it in bed each night for two weeks. Words that had seemed pretty easy to say when I was alone now came out in a stammer.

He said something that I didn't get, so I said, "I'm sorry. Would you mind repeating that?"

He did what so many people do. Instead of repeating it, he said, "It wasn't important. Never mind."

I think he said that some changes are for the better, but I'll never know for sure. I sometimes resented people's deciding for me what was and wasn't worth repeating. They were sort of like unofficial censors. Thinking about that, though, had the effect of making me less nervous about the Belonging Plan.

Then he said, "You can't understand half of what I say, can you? It must be rough." He looked like he really cared, and when something in his eyes told me he understood, I felt a surge of gratitude.

"Sometimes yes, sometimes no." I told him. My eyes left his face and dropped to my hands as I tacked on, "I'm sorry."

"That's right, Gustie," I told myself. *"Apologize—again—for being a pain in the neck to other people. For being deaf. For being you."*

I felt tears blurring my eyes, a much too common thing since my illness. I blinked them away. But I still felt like my feelings were bottled up and ready to explode.

"Some things you can do without words," I think Tony said.

"*Yeah*," I thought. "*Things like ping pong, shampooing your hair, kicking your locker door when it sticks . . . kissing.*" But I didn't say any of this out loud.

Tony's eyes changed from a milk chocolate brown to that almost black-brown of a Hershey's semi-sweet piece. I wondered what he was thinking.

Before I really guessed what he was going to do, he said, I think, "Things like this."

What a time not to understand somebody!

Very gently, he tipped my chin up, hypnotized me with those Hershey's semi-sweet eyes, and leaned close to kiss me.

I almost pulled away and bagged my Belonging Plan right then and there. I didn't like Tony Riach as a boyfriend. Or did I? Maybe I ought to because he'd agreed to be with me. "*Little Miss Grateful*," I scolded myself. I wanted his kiss, didn't I, to prove . . . to prove what? The answer wasn't clear to me now.

Seconds passed with our lips still meshed together. He eased me back against a soft bed of maple leaves. It smelled woodsy all around, but I was more aware of Tony's clean, soapy scent. I wondered if he smelled my cologne. He kissed me again, and again.

Part of me wanted to shout "Stop!" But even more, I wanted to be close to someone. Being close was what I wanted, wasn't it? I didn't need to hear to be this close to someone. I belonged as much as a hearing girl.

But just when I thought I knew what it was to belong, I knew in an instant that it was wrong for me. I knew that I wasn't ready for this, that I didn't even like Tony as a boyfriend.

I would have to try to tell him.

"Tony," I said.

He must have thought I was saying his name passionately. I'm not sure what he said. Suddenly, Tony's kisses were more forceful.

"No, Tony, no. Please stop! I can't."

He didn't listen. He seemed deaf. But then all of a sudden he stopped. He swore—I think—and stood up and turned his back to me for a minute.

"Let's go," he said.

The ride back seemed very long and quiet. I was sure my face was a tomato-red reflection of my regret and embarrassment. When Tony finally parked in front of my house, I said, "Tony, whatever you think, I'm not a tease. I've never done anything like this before. I'm . . . I'm very sorry." My eyes begged him to understand.

To my relief, he took my hand and said, "I think I understand. It's okay. No one will ever know but us. Stay true to yourself." Then he was gone.

In bed that night, I realized how stupid my Belonging Plan had been. I realized that I'd never belong if I threw away my innermost values and beliefs.

Lenore

·

While I was looking in my book bag for my yellow highlighter pen one day, my hand brushed against something jammed into one corner. It had a funny feel I didn't recognize. Puzzled, I pulled it out.

It was Mr. Tate's handkerchief. I'd had it for three months!

"You don't have to pretend with me." The special education teacher's words came back to me as I looked at the bunched-up piece of cloth.

Isn't pretending what I'd been doing? Pretending to still be Sara's good listener. Pretending to understand in school. Pretending I didn't see the tension between Mom and Dad over my hearing loss. Pretending that I was the same me as before I had meningitis.

"Stay true to yourself," Tony had said.

But who was I? That was the trouble. I wasn't sure.

I looked again at Mr. Tate's mascara-stained handkerchief. Then I washed it.

Mr. Tate was sitting at his desk when I knocked on his partly open office door. He smiled when he looked up and saw me. I saw then that he was on the phone. That made me feel funny. Should I just stand there in the doorway, or should I walk in? It wasn't as if I'd overhear any of his conversation. He settled it for me when he motioned for me to come in and sit down.

I kept myself busy looking at his posters. Most of them were large travel posters like you see in travel agencies. There was one of Dubrovnik, Yugoslavia, another of Luxor, Egypt, and one of some unlabeled sunny island that I didn't recognize. Not matching the travel poster theme was another poster that said, "When life hands you a lemon, make lemonade."

I was looking at that one when Mr. Tate hung up the phone.

"I like your posters," I told him.

"Thanks. Without a window in this cubbyhole, I needed a little color." As he said this, he walked around the edge of his desk and sat on its front corner. Then he said, "How are you doing? I'm glad to see you."

I wondered what he would think if I told him I was doing awful. My best friend had dumped me. I had almost done something stupid with Tony Riach. My folks and I weren't communicating, and school was driving me crazy.

Putting off answering his question, I said, "I brought back your handkerchief," as I pulled it out of my purse. I'd ironed it into a crisp little square. The mascara spots had washed out.

As he took it from me, his warm eyes and friendly smile encouraged me to talk.

You don't have to pretend with me.

Swallowing a strange lump in my throat, I said, "Mr. Tate, I didn't come just to bring back your handkerchief. I really came to talk." I hesitated, swallowing hard, and added, "But I don't know what it is that I came here to talk about. I guess that sounds crazy."

"Not really. Lots of things are hard to put into words. I take it life has been on the downswing?"

"To put it mildly," I agreed, giving him a little smile that I wasn't really sure of.

"Is it school in particular, or is it just sort of Everything with a capital E?"

His "Everything with a capital E" brought a smile I was sure of. It summed up my situation so well. My whole life seemed pretty screwed up.

"Everything with a capital E," I told him.

His answering nod made me feel better, too. He said, "Well, then

. . ." He seemed to drop one line of thought to pick up another. "You know, I think the only way to tackle an Everything situation is to take it apart and try to solve one thing at a time. The Everything then gradually becomes less."

"That sounds like a good idea. But where do I start with an Everything?" It seemed to be so complicated. My parents. Feeling like one big set of ears. Lost friendships. School. Then I answered my own question, saying, "I think I know. Miss Hartman told me that you might know some ways to make school easier for me. Maybe that's a good place to start."

Nodding, he said, "You've come to the right guy. Tell me how you've been handling the school situation."

"Well," I admitted, "I've been pretending a lot. A teacher will call on me, for example, and sometimes I play dumb because I'm too embarrassed to ask her to say it again. So I just pretend like I don't know the answer."

Once more he nodded, as though he didn't think faking it was so odd. I felt encouraged to continue.

"I do okay on test questions that come right from the textbook. If it's something from class discussion, though, I'm often lost. I try so hard to speechread, Mr. Tate, but teachers walk back and forth across the room or turn away or talk very fast. Some of them have lips that just don't move much when they talk. Even if I'm lucky and follow well, I can't write anything down in my notebook and watch the teacher at the same time."

"Go on," he said.

"I want very much to be in on everything, but I really get tired from concentrating so hard. I know most teachers—oh dear . . ."

"You maybe forgot for a minute that I'm a teacher?"

"Yes."

"Say it anyway. Not all of us are alike."

"Well, what I was going to say is that most teachers usually don't say anything earthshaking. They just comment on what's in the book. But I care, Mr. Tate. I want to know what's going on. I get the feeling that my teachers are adding a little something, maybe from their own lives, that makes the stuff in the book stand out. Maybe these things won't show up on a test, but the hearing kids get to sort them out and I don't. I feel cheated sometimes. I feel so . . . shut out."

My chest felt tight and my eyes were burning. Was I going to need his handkerchief again?

When I didn't say more right away, he said, "Well, Gustie, I think I've got some good news for you. I think there's a way you can feel more included again."

"How?" I asked a little shakily. This sounded so good. Did he really have an answer that would work?

"Would you give me your permission to line up some student notetakers?"

"Notetakers?" I asked. "But they wouldn't want to share their notes with me, would they, or go to the bother?"

"I don't see why not."

"But . . ." "*That will make me different,*" I thought. "*But you are different. You need help.*"

"But?" he prodded.

The biggest smile I'd had for a long time popped out from nowhere. "I'll try it!"

Mr. Tate really helped me a lot. He found someone to take notes for me in each of my classes. They all turned out to be a big help, but Lenore O'Malley was special from the start.

Lenore hit the high points of class discussion in her notes, and she made sure I knew assignments and test dates. She also peppered her notes with the little extras—those little things I had been missing that make a class come alive. She put in the class jokes and stories, for one thing. And, she put in the odd bits of information: *Maybe the Titanic sank because there was a curse connected with a mummy aboard the ship.* One time after writing down a long assignment, she drew a Mr. Yuk sketch.

Day by day, I got to know Lenore through her notes. I liked her. She was bright, she had a sense of humor, and she had a way of knowing the really big points of a lecture. She drew a star beside the most important things. I felt more relaxed in class with her there.

My other notetakers were not as good as Lenore. One of them was fine about writing down the key points, for instance, but he always left out those little things that I missed. He also had the bad habit of forgetting to let me know if a teacher changed an assignment or a test date. While Lenore would fill in a block of classtime with the notation that Mr. Railsback was telling the same joke he told last week, my other helpers would just stop writing. I always wondered what I was missing, and sometimes I felt alone and upset.

Lenore had been in some of my classes since junior high. Back then, everyone used to call her Four-by-Four Lenore because she was fat. You'd never guess it now, though. She had a really nice figure. It's just that people who knew her when she was fat still seemed to think of her as Four-by-Four Lenore. They didn't take the time to get to know her for herself.

The kids in junior high really gave her a bad time. They talked about elephants and blubber and played some practical jokes on her. Although I hadn't thought up any of the names or jokes, to be in, I'd laughed along with most of them. I felt awfully guilty about that now.

One time in junior high, for example, John Saylor put a Twinkie on Lenore's chair. An unsuspecting Lenore, loaded down with books and her own body weight, plopped onto the Twinkie-rigged chair. Naturally, everybody cracked up. Now, it no longer seemed funny. In fact, it was cruel. How could we have done it? Any one of us, including me, could have taken the Twinkie off the chair or warned Lenore, but it had seemed like harmless fun at the time.

Lenore had handled the situation well. She had shown us up and made us look immature. Instead of crying or making a fuss, she sat on the Twinkie all hour, no doubt aware that the cream filling was seeping through her skirt. She must have felt like dying.

And now she was being friendly and helpful to me. That niceness had probably been there all along.

"You can make friends when you least expect to," my mother often said. I had a feeling she was right.

Lenore and I began seeing each other outside of school. She told me that she liked her brother's best friend and hoped he'd ask her out sooner or later. In the meantime, she wasn't dating anybody special.

I told her about the Belonging Plan and that there wasn't anybody special asking me out either.

She told me how her dad had died of cancer. When she cried, I comforted her.

I told her that Gordon Blaine wasn't my biological father. I didn't remember my biological father at all; he died when I was a baby. When Mom married Gordon Blaine, he adopted me. He's the only father I've known and I felt like he was my real father. Lenore understood.

I told her how I liked classical music. When she asked me if I missed it, I cried and she comforted me.

She told me she liked opera, and I listened to her reasons.

We agreed that we both had old-fashioned names. We decided that it was kind of fun to be named after a favorite ancestor.

We talked about all kinds of things. After sharing lots of secrets, I finally felt like I knew her well enough to apologize for the junior-high Twinkie prank. To my surprise, Lenore laughed about it.

"It hurt an awful lot at the time," she admitted, "but it wasn't so terrible. I can even get a mental picture of my huge behind turning a Twinkie into mush and laugh at it." Her laugh changed into a slight frown as she looked off into space for a minute before adding, "In some ways, Gustie, there are two of me. There's a fat me and this me," she said, pointing to her now slender form. "I have to work hard to stay slim. Picturing myself squashing that Twinkie helps me stay this way.

"The worst thing about being fat was feeling that I didn't belong. In gym, no one wanted me on their team. I wasn't into trying a lot of different makeup or wearing cute little designer jeans."

I think my mouth dropped open. *Two of her; didn't belong*—that's exactly how I felt about myself.

"You look surprised," she told me.

"Wow, Lenore, I am. I understand better than you know." I explained my own feelings of not fitting in and there being two of me.

Our honesty encouraged me to ask her something that had been on my mind. "You are so patient with me. Doesn't it bother you when I stumble over a word and you have to say it again? Why do you put up with me?"

"Because I really like you, silly."

"Because my being deaf makes me a . . . a, well, underdog?"

"Well, sort of. I guess you remind me of myself. There are many ways to be handicapped. All of us are in some way, but sometimes it takes something like being fat or deaf to see it. I was handicapped when I was fat. I still am because I'm afraid."

"Afraid?"

"I don't have a lot of friends, Gustie. I think some people still see me as a nerd. Someone has even been leaving pictures of Miss Piggy on my locker door. That hurts. My new friends . . . oh, I guess it sounds silly and like I'm feeling sorry for myself."

"No, it doesn't. Please tell me," I encouraged, touching her hand lightly.

"I worry that they'd drop me if I gained back all that weight. It seems like I was punished for being different, for being fat. Now that I look normal, people like me better. I guess I don't embarrass them anymore. What I want more than anything else is to be accepted for myself, for what's inside me that no one can see with their eyes, something that's there no matter if I'm fat or thin."

My eyes puddled up with feeling. I put my hands on Lenore's shoulders, looked into her eyes, and said, "I won't ever drop you, friend."

Black Thursday

•

To my surprise, one day in April, Dana Arlington asked me to stop at Jacob's, the burger shop near school, to have a Coke with her.

I was standing at my locker thinking about the big history test Mr. Railsback had just announced for the day after tomorrow. All those dates! But at least I knew about this test. A couple of times notetakers had forgotten to let me know.

When I felt a light tap on my shoulder, I jumped. I don't know what I expected to find behind me, but when you don't hear somebody coming and they're suddenly there with a tap, it's weird.

When I turned around and saw Dana standing there, I smiled, but it was odd to see her. I wondered if I looked as surprised as I felt. Although she was in one of my classes, we hadn't done anything together since I'd been sick. In fact, she had only come to visit me at home that one time with Sara to drop off my books.

"Hi, Dana. How are you doing?"

She was moving her load of notebooks and things from the crook of one arm to the other, then back again. Then she held up a forefinger and mouthed "wait" while she fished a piece of paper out of her purse.

She handed the paper to me as if it were something to be proud of. It read:

Would you like to have a Coke with me today at Jacob's?

Lots of things went through my mind. I remembered her conversation with Sara behind the bush that day I overheard them talking about my hearing, and I almost didn't go to Jacob's. But then I also remembered the good times we'd had, and I decided to give it a try. I'd only be hurting myself if I avoided people. To tell you the truth, now that I'd had the benefit of speechreading lessons and lots of practice, I wanted to dazzle Dana with a display of my speechreading ability. I knew now that Dana's speech was pretty easy to read, but she only remembered that time at the house right after I was sick when I had to depend on faulty hearing.

After stopping at a phone booth to have Dana call my mom to let her know I'd be late, we walked to the burger place. I did practically all the talking because I figured this wasn't the place to dazzle Dana. I knew if I tried to read her lips and walk at the same time, I might end up on the ground. My balance still wasn't as good as it used to be, and I had to concentrate as I walked.

After we'd gotten a table and had been served our Cokes, I saw that she was writing me another note. I didn't know whether to feel pleased or insulted that she felt I had to read notes.

"Dana, I appreciate the notes, but I've learned a lot about reading lips since that time at my house," I told her. "Maybe I'll do better at talking if we give it another try."

Her writing hand stopped in midair and for a few seconds she didn't seem to understand what I'd just said. Then she put down her pen and said, "I'm sorry. I feel stupid." She hung her head like a scolded puppy and then raised it as she added, "Did you understand what I just said? You know, about being sorry?"

"You bet I did, Dana, and if you look right at me when you talk, I think we'll do just fine." Wanting to encourage her, I told her, "You speak very clearly."

"Thanks."

"Are you almost ready for Railsback's test?" I asked, wanting to change a subject I could tell was embarrassing her.

"Well, no, actually I'm not." When she stopped, I noticed that she was shredding her napkin. "That's the main reason I asked you if we could have a Coke today."

What did she mean? I thought she just wanted to get together and talk about guys and clothes and all the things we used to talk about.

"What do you mean?" I asked. Then I knew, and it felt like somebody had just turned off a light inside me.

"Well," she explained, "I missed four days of school when I had the flu. This is my first day back, and I'm really lost with this test coming up."

When she paused as though waiting for me to say something, I didn't. I felt so cruddy.

"I know you have a notetaker, and I was wondering if—um—if I could maybe copy your notes for the days I wasn't there."

Normally I would have been happy to share my notes, but Dana had practically ignored me for months. I suddenly realized that the only reason she was having a Coke with me was because she wanted something from me. I felt terrible. I was so hurt that I handed her my notebook without saying anything. As I watched her copy the notes, I began to think that maybe I was jumping to conclusions. I had decided too fast that she was just using me. Surely we'd have a nice talk after she'd gotten done.

But just as she was about finished, in walked a bunch of girls. Although only a few short months ago, I would have been glad to see them coming toward our table, everything felt different now. I would have liked to talk just to Dana. I no longer had that automatic feeling of belonging to this group. When I noticed that Sara was with them, I felt awful.

Nothing in common.

The memory of our conversation at her house still hurt like crazy, but I wasn't going to let Sara know.

They pulled up chairs to our table. I didn't follow every word of conversation, In a group, I had to be quick with my eyes to see who tossed the talk to whom. It was like not knowing where a ball was going to be thrown next. I often missed part of the talk because it took a while for me to find the newest speaker. It was also easy to lose the thread of conversation when somebody changed the topic. You know how it goes. One subject leads to another, but if you don't hear, you miss the lead-in to a new subject. A switch from, say, makeup to reincarnation isn't very logical. Knowing the topic makes speechreading much easier. It give you clues.

At one point, I lost the thread of the conversation, but to my surprise, I felt good. I laughed and smiled along with the others even when I didn't know why they were smiling. In this case, it wasn't pretending. I wasn't trying to put one over on anybody. I just felt happy inside to see them having a good time. I was feeling their mood, if not their actual thoughts and the words they said.

My mind drifted into a silent thank you for feeling joy in others' pleasure. To me right then, it seemed to be the nitty-gritty—my English teacher would say the *essence*—of a laugh or a smile.

I must have had a dreamy look on my face. Sara suddenly got my attention by waving her arms in front of my face. When I looked at her, she said, "Gustie, why are you sitting there grinning like a monkey?"

"Just daydreaming a little," I told her. I wasn't going to let Sara Marler take away my peacefulness.

"Well, you look dopey smiling when we're talking about World War III. Or are you so wrapped up in your little self that the idea of nuclear war doesn't matter?"

I didn't know why she was talking to me like that. Her snotty look and words hit me like a punch in the stomach. I guess I'd really missed an important switch of topic that time. How had the conversation gone so quickly from something that made everybody smile to something as awful as nuclear war?

I noticed that everyone was staring at me, waiting for me to answer Sara's question. Nobody took a bite of anything. Nobody took a swig of pop. Nobody even moved.

Squeezing my hands together in my lap, I tried to make my voice icy but dignified as I said, "I'm sorry it bothers you, Sara. It's something I can't really help."

Wanting to change the direction of the conversation and have some fun again at the table, I tried tossing the conversational ball to Cindy.

"Cindy, that's really neat about your bro . . . "

Sara cut me off. "We already talked about his anchoring the evening news," she informed me, as if my not knowing made me a dunce.

I felt like running out of the restaurant. This wasn't fair to me, and it wasn't even fair to the rest of the people at the table.

"Sara," I told her, "why don't we save our personal differences for when just the two of us are together?" *Please*, Sara, my eyes tried to plead.

"That would be difficult. You're always with Twinkie Pants."

"Twinkie Pants?"

"Four-by-Four."

"Sara, her name is Lenore. Give yourself a chance to know her. She's very nice. She doesn't deserve those names." "*I don't either*," I thought, wondering what Sara called me behind my back.

Then Sara said something that I didn't get. When I asked her to please repeat it, she refused. Dana jumped up then and said something to Sara. I couldn't see Dana's mouth because her back was to me, but I could tell they'd begun to argue.

"This must be my exit cue," I told the group as I started walking out. I had to leave before I dumped Cindy's chocolate soda over Sara's head. I really felt like it.

I was standing just outside the restaurant's door, trying to decide if I wanted to walk all the way home or catch a bus, when Sara came out. Fortunately, the soda was out of reach.

"*Ignore her*," I thought. But I said, "Sara, what is the matter with you? You used to be so nice and thoughtful. Hurting me is one thing, but I won't stand by and see you hurt Lenore."

Then all of a sudden, something occurred to me. I hoped I was wrong, but I felt I had to ask Sara. "It was you who left the Miss Piggy pictures on her locker, wasn't it?"

I could tell by the look on her face that it was, and it chilled me to see that Sara looked almost proud of it.

"Four-by-Four," she said.

"Stop that stupid, childish name calling."

"You used to go along with it," she taunted.

"Yeah, *used to*, Sara, before I knew better. Why don't you grow up?"

"Why are you doing this to me?"

"Doing what to you?" I asked. The question puzzled me.

"Picking on me."

"What? Me pick on you! Sara, you pick on everybody. You pick on people less fortunate than you are. You pick on people you've decided aren't as good as you are. But that's not all. You're nasty to popular people, too, if they seem to threaten your superiority. You have to be the 'bestest,'" I told her, using one of her little girl words, "the bestest one around."

"I'm not going to listen to . . . "

"Yes, you are," I told her angrily.

Then I saw something that changed my mood. My anger left as suddenly as air leaving a punctured balloon. I felt my chest tighten with sadness when I saw a look in her eyes that I'd seen so many times since we were five-year-olds sharing Barbies and secrets. There was no way that I could forget the past, our years of friendship, and Sara's basic niceness that had gotten lost somewhere along the line lately.

But I also liked Lenore. In a voice that I hoped was gentler than before, but firm, I said, "Sara, please leave Lenore alone. She's nice. She's had a rough time."

She gave me a look that said maybe she would and maybe she wouldn't.

And then it happened.

Without any warning, Sara bolted out into the street.

"Watch out!" I shouted.

I had the sensation of hearing the impact as the car struck her body, only I knew I was imagining the sound.

Horror-struck, I watched Sara's body arc through the air and land against the curb.

New Guy On Campus

·

Sara has a broken rib, some cuts, and a very sore body," Mom told me after talking to Sara's mother on the phone.

"Poor Sara. What can we do to help her now?"

"Let's send some flowers," Mom suggested. "She can't have visitors right away."

I wasn't sure Sara would want to see me anyway. Remembering our argument, I wished I hadn't said any of those things to her. I wanted her to get better fast.

"I feel so guilty," I told my parents, explaining what had happened right before the accident. "We were arguing. Then she ran right out into the street without even looking."

I couldn't shake off the awful feeling that Sara hadn't cared if a car was coming.

"She was upset," Dad said as he patted my hand and patiently repeated what I didn't get. His thin lips continued to challenge me, although I was getting better at understanding him. "We've all had some close calls in traffic, one way or another," he continued. "Sara was more unfortunate that most of us because there was a car coming just when she was careless."

All week, Mrs. Marler gave Mom daily reports on Sara's slow but steady progress in the hospital. My parents continued to help me get over the feeling that the accident was my fault. I guess they got through to me. I realized that what really mattered wasn't who got the blame. It was just having Sara heal.

For the first few days after the accident, everybody at school seemed to be talking about it. By the fourth day, though, Sara was better, and talk died down. Everyone still cared and was interested in how she was doing, but other things came first once again, in the "life goes on" way.

The other main topic of the week, according to Lenore, was a new guy who had just transferred to Central. From what she'd heard people say, he was dreamy.

I hadn't especially wanted to meet him. Sara was on my mind most of the time. Plus, I was still trying to forget that awful Belonging Plan with Tony Riach, who, luckily for me, acted as he always had before our ride. As far as I knew, Tony had kept his promise and not told anyone about our weird Saturday afternoon.

Thanks to Lenore, I met the new guy anyway.

"That's him," Lenore said one day just outside the school library. She motioned off to her left, where all I could see was a side view of a guy with dark hair, a well-built body, and nice clothes.

Then he turned. To my surprise, he wasn't a mysterious stranger at all. Eyes as blue as my Siamese cat's met mine, and we recognized each other instantly.

"I know him," I whispered to Lenore. At least, I hoped it was a whisper. Sometimes I forgot that I'd lost my normal volume control; what was meant to be a whisper could be loud enough for everyone close to hear. "I'll tell you more later," I added quickly.

He walked toward us, and suddenly he was only two feet away. "Gustie? Gustie Blaine?"

"Jack. Yes, it's me. I'm so glad to see you." I was really happy that he remembered me. I knew Jack Reilly only from our brief meeting on the beach last summer.

I introduced Jack and Lenore. I could tell Lenore was dying to hear how we'd met, but after the introduction, she tactfully went back into the library, leaving Jack and me alone.

We sat on a nearby bench.

"Every time I hear *Rhapsody in Blue*, I think of you and that perfect summer day," he told me.

It hit me right then with a giant thud that I'd never hear *Rhapsody in Blue* again. My final memory of it would be on the radio that day at the beach right before I got sick.

"I wish I could say the same," I said. I felt a lump catch in my throat and wondered if he'd heard it in my voice.

It was never easy to face what was gone, like music, or to tell someone that I was deaf. I wanted to be honest with Jack, but I was afraid I'd see the light of interest in his eyes flicker out.

I told him anyway. He didn't back away or seem to pity me, like so many people did at first. Neither did he seem self-conscious as I concentrated on reading his full, bow-shaped lips.

"It's great to see you, Gustie. I was kind of hoping I'd run into you. My mom and I moved here last week. My parents just got divorced, and my dad took a job overseas, so Mom decided to sell the house and move here. My brother and sister-in-law live here, too. I was visiting them last summer when I met you.

"Do you think we could get together some time, you know, for dinner or something?"

"Sure!" I answered. I hoped my voice didn't sound as excited as I felt, but at that point, I didn't really care. I was ecstatic knowing that Jack wanted to go out with me, even if I was deaf. The walk home that afternoon flew by in record time.

Jack and I began spending a lot of time together. Unlike some really good-looking guys, Jack didn't seem like a phony. It was strange about us. Although we hardly knew each other, it didn't seem that way. I felt very relaxed when I was with Jack—free to be myself.

"Doesn't it bother you that I'm deaf?" I asked him one day. I was surprised when that popped out. Until now, I'd only asked Lenore that question.

"It's weird, Gustie," he told me without hesitation. "I know you're deaf, but I don't really think of you that way. You're just someone special I like to be with. Your hearing loss is just a part of the whole package, like your bright eyes."

My cheeks felt warm with pleasure; I must have turned bright red.

"You've very special to feel that way," I told him.

"Well, to tell you the truth, I don't deserve any special marks for accepting you." He gave me a sheepish smile and admitted, "I've had a lifetime of practice."

"What do you mean?"

"My older brother Larry is deaf and so is his wife."

"Honestly?" I asked. Boy, was I surprised. I guess I hadn't thought there were any other deaf people living in my town. It really seemed too coincidental, but also sort of nice, that Jack's brother was one of them. "No wonder you've had a lifetime of practice."

"Yeah, well, I kind of couldn't help it. But, deaf people are different from each other, you know. They are individuals with individual needs. Not all deaf people can speechread like you do, Gustie. Some of them use sign language. Larry does, and so do I when I'm with him. But being deaf doesn't mean that you have to sign.

"There are a lot of deaf people who don't sign. Many of them are like you—they lost their hearing when they were teenagers or adults. You have an advantage; you know what speech sounds like, so your memory gives you clues when you speechread.

"Larry was born deaf, so he has never heard speech. His first language was sign language. Larry knows how to talk, but he usually doesn't because he thinks people can't understand him. He seems to get along okay, though. Some of the other technicians at the lab where he works have learned some signs, and others just write notes to him. Larry doesn't care how people communicate with him as long as they try."

Jack helped me a lot with my feelings about being deaf. When I told him about my parents' attitude of silence on the topic of my hearing loss, Jack even seemed to understand that.

"Sometimes my parents look so sad, Jack. It makes me feel guilty for being different than I used to be. I want to hug them, to comfort them, but sometimes I freeze up. I start feeling very angry and scared about feeling shut out. Sometimes I wonder if they still love me."

"I think I understand your parents' reaction."

"You do?"

He nodded his head and looked right into my eyes. "In a way, maybe your parents are grieving. Once in a while, my mother talks about her feelings when she found out Larry couldn't hear. It was a shock at first, but it didn't make her stop loving him.

"I bet every parent dreams of having a perfect baby. Nobody is perfect, but the illusion is there—ten little toes, ten perfect little fingers, and so on. Larry seemed like a perfect baby to Mom until she noticed that he wasn't talking like other kids his age. In a way, she had to mourn the loss of this dream of perfection and find a new definition of *normal*. What is normal anyway? Mom found out that it goes a lot deeper than having ten fingers, or hearing, or seeing, or being able to walk down the street."

Jack took my hand very gently. "Your parents love you as much as before. Maybe they love you even more now, Gustie, since they almost lost you. Give them time."

I'd never thought of it that way. What he said made sense. Maybe my getting sick was extra hard on my parents because they had medical training. Even so, it wasn't their fault that they didn't know right away how sick I was. And even though Dad's a doctor, it wasn't his fault that he couldn't heal me. Maybe they just needed time to work out all their feelings. I promised myself to be more patient with my parents.

Jack and I didn't talk about my hearing all the time. We discussed school, our favorite books and movies, and our hopes and dreams. We found out that we had a lot in common.

Jack even had trouble understanding *his* parents.

"You said sometimes you wonder if your parents still love you," he told me one afternoon. He bowed his head for a moment and shook it, and then he looked back at me so I could read his lips. "Sometimes I wonder if mine ever really loved me."

I could feel my forehead wrinkle into a frown, Jack usually seemed so confident; his doubt surprised me.

"What do you mean?" I asked, not sure what he was getting at.

"Maybe it sounds crazy," he told me, "but sometimes I think my parents should have gotten divorced a long time ago. They say they stayed together as long as they did for Larry and me; but Gustie, I think we'd have been better off if they hadn't."

That seemed strange to me, because I thought kids were better off if their parents stayed together. Now, from what Jack was saying, it seemed that maybe this wasn't always true. In what I hoped was a soft, encouraging voice, I said, "I'd like to hear about it if you want to talk about it."

"It's hard to know where to start. I get the feeling that maybe if they'd separated years ago, they'd still have some respect for each other. They might at least have stayed friends. But they stayed together. It's like all the arguing, all Mom's weird silences—the whole thing—chipped away little by little at whatever love they had, until now there's nothing left. I used to hear them fight. It's bad enough for any kid to hear parents going at each other, but the thing that got me was one of them would say something like, 'I can't take this anymore. If it weren't for the boys, I'd be gone.'"

Jack looked off into space, like he was hearing it all over again. Then he looked at me again.

"Do you know how I felt and still feel sometimes?" he asked. "Like I trapped them into staying together just by being a kid. The arguing got worse and worse and then it almost stopped. They just didn't say anything to each other, except stuff like 'Please pass the salt.' I think the coldness was even worse that the fights. They're bitter, Gustie, and it seems like my fault."

It looked like his voice broke, I didn't want to say anything yet in case he needed to say more. I put all the compassion I felt into a gentle touch of his cheek. It seemed to be just the right thing to do. While my hand was still there, he put his large one over mine and pressed it hard against the softness of his face.

He seemed to be all talked out, so I said, "It's not your fault, Jack. They did what they thought was best for you and Larry. You can't know what their lives would have been like if they'd gotten a divorce a long time ago. Maybe they needed to try to keep their marriage together for themselves, too. This way they know they tried. But it wasn't your fault. Give them time and maybe some of the bitterness will go away."

"I don't know. You really think so?" The hand that had been on his cheek had moved down to my side. Now he touched it lightly with his fingers. "Thanks for listening. It's not something I can talk about with just anyone."

A little something inside me sang. It felt so good to be able to help him, even that tiny bit.

Jack also helped me rediscover music. One afternoon we walked to his house after school to pick up a book. I had to write a term paper on the Civil War, and Jack was sure his mother had a book that would help me.

Two walls of the living room were lined with built-in bookcases, but Jack easily found the thick volume he had in mind. Just as he handed it to me, he told me the phone was ringing.

"Be right back," said Jack as he moved toward the hallway. A minute later he was back. "Gustie, I have to run next door to do a favor for my neighbor. Why don't you leaf through that book or browse through the shelves for a few minutes while I'm gone?"

Glad to have the chance to look more closely at Mrs. Reilly's library, I told him it was fine. Right after he left, a strange thing happened. When I turned to put the heavy Civil War book on a coffee table, I saw the piano on the other side of the room. I hadn't noticed it before.

I sort of froze. I can't really explain what happened after that. I moved like a sleepwalker toward the piano and sat down on its bench.

Without really deciding to, I put my hands above the keyboard. They stayed suspended there until I broke the spell with a deep breath.

And then my fingers were moving through the piano solo of *Rhapsody in Blue*.

I had not forgotten how to play. My ears were as deaf as ever and I couldn't hear a single note I played, and yet I did hear. I heard the music so clearly in my memory and through the vibrations in the piano keys and the wood. Even my feet seemed to have ears as they felt vibrations tingling their way through the hardwood floor.

When I struck the pounding chords of one passage, all my bottled-up frustrations gushed out of the corners of my eyes. When I played a difficult passage, I liked myself again. And when I came to the main theme, I gasped in recognition.

Life was good. It was no less good now than it used to be. It was just different. The music made me feel like I belonged and was like other people. The music spoke to me in its wordless language, and I heard it with a feeling rather than with two ears. As I played, I felt strong and healed.

I didn't realize that I was crying tears of joy until I played the final notes. I must have looked like an idiot, crying and grinning at the same time, but I felt better than I had in a long, long time.

That's how Jack found me when he returned. Fortunately, he understood my emotions.

"How long were you there?" I asked him.

"Long enough to know you haven't lost your touch." He looked almost as if he would cry, too, as he added, "Gustie, that was beautiful."

"Thank you for helping me find music again, Jack."

"You never really lost it, you know."

Maybe I hadn't.

He sat down beside me on the piano bench, and when he kissed me for the first time, it was very tender and sweet.

Blossoming

•

"How's the weather up there?" Lenore asked. We were taking a break from studying for a big Latin test.

"What?" I asked. I didn't know if I'd read her lips right.

"How's the weather up there?"

I had read the sentence right, after all, but I still didn't know what she meant.

"Up where?"

"Cloud Nine."

Suddenly understanding, I grinned and said, "Is it that obvious?" I wondered if people who fell in love wore special smiles to clue in others.

"To me it is. You've got this certain glow."

"Oh, Lenore," I sighed. The memory of *Rhapsody in Blue* and Jack's kiss had put me on another plane. "Jack is really special." And then I told her all the reasons why.

"Small world," Lenore commented when I mentioned that Jack had grown up with a deaf brother. Then, after I'd told her everything, she said. "Jack really sounds understanding, Gustie."

In a rush of enthusiasm, I said, "Oh, he is. He's just so natural with me, Lenore. My not hearing isn't some kind of wall between us."

"I'm so glad," she told me, and I knew she really meant it by the way her eyes softened. Another kind of friend might have been jealous, but not Lenore.

Her happiness for me led me to confide, "He kissed me."

"Tell me more." We were sitting on the floor in her room, and as she said this, she plumped up the pillows behind her back as if waiting for a long, detailed story.

"It was . . . tender . . . sweet," I told her, searching for words to describe the gentle, beautiful feeling. "He wasn't all slobbery and gropey. You know how lots of guys try to be friendly, all just leading up to the main event—kissing and stuff." Lenore nodded. "But with Jack, the kiss was just one more very special part of everything that goes together to make us friends. Do you know what I mean?"

Nodding again, Lenore said, "You're so lucky, Gustie."

"I know."

It was a beautiful May Saturday. Jack and I had planned on going to the movies, but we decided the day was too nice to spend inside a dark theater.

"We ought to take advantage of this weather," he said as we walked toward his mother's car. A gentle breeze played through the lilac bushes and blew their scent our way.

"I totally agree," I said, inhaling the wonderful fragrance. "What should it be? A walk somewhere? A ride through the countryside? Hey, I know; why don't I pack a picnic basket? Even if we're not hungry now, we will be later."

"That sounds great. And who says we're not hungry now?" he added with a wink.

So we turned around and went back into the house. Mom was standing at the kitchen sink. "Did you forget something?"

"No, Mrs. Blaine. We decided it's too great a day to waste on a movie."

"It must be 75° at least," Mom said, nodding her head in agreement.

"Is it okay if I take some stuff out of the fridge to make a picnic basket?" I asked.

"Of course. Anything but the food for Sunday dinner. There's some fried chicken left from last night. I thought I'd take advantage of the gorgeous weather, too," she said, pointing to the small clippers she had just oiled, "by working in the flower beds a little. Have a good time."

We quickly put a feast together, got in the car, and took off. We decided to drive to Michigan City, which isn't in Michigan like you may think. It's in Indiana, on the south shore of Lake Michigan. There's a pretty harbor, sand dunes, and a gray-green expanse of the lake. Before eating, we walked around the harbor area, which was still half-empty because the boating season was just beginning. We saw lots of boats in drydock. Here and there, boat owners were scraping and sanding.

"Do you want to try the breakwater?" Jack asked. *Breakwater* was a toughie to speechread, but Jack pointed to it as he repeated his question, and I understood that time.

The breakwater was a long cement structure, not too wide, that jutted out into the lake. It had a light at its tip to guide the boats safely into harbor. I'd been on it dozens of times because I loved the lake breeze. I also liked going out to the breakwater's end to try to spot interesting boats coming in, like the red Chinese junk that often sailed in and out of the harbor.

But now, considering that my balance had never gotten all the way back to normal, the breakwater seemed narrower and longer than I remembered it. I wouldn't have dreamed of going out there alone or with just anyone. But this was Jack beside me, and I really felt safe with him. He had probably anticipated that I might not want to try it, and somehow I knew he'd understand if I said I wasn't ready. Instead, I told him I'd try it if he would hang onto me.

Even though he held my arm to steady me and walked closer to the edge than I did, I didn't feel too sure of myself. It really hit me how different I was from the days when I'd skipped along the breakwater's length. The water's deep, so I'd always been careful then, but I could talk and walk at the same time or look out at the passing boats as I made my way toward the little lighthouse at the end.

Now I had to concentrate on putting one foot in front of the other. Even though I knew Jack wouldn't let me fall, I kept thinking I would. When we were about a third of the way down the breakwater, I said, "Let's stop and sit down." I was starting to feel dizzy.

We sat with our faces to the harbor entrance. For a little while I felt pretty sorry for myself, comparing this day to those other ones when I'd cavorted down the breakwater like a sure-footed colt. What was I now? For a minute, I pictured myself as a clumsy Godzilla, and the idea made me laugh out loud.

"What's so funny?" Jack asked. The wind was blowing his dark hair this way and that; his blue eyes invited me to share my feelings.

When I explained the comparison between my old coltish self and my present self, he laughed along with me.

But shaking his head for emphasis, he told me, "Godzilla you're not."

I was glad that he didn't think of me that way. More serious again, I asked, "Do you think my balance will ever be like it used to be?"

Jack paused as if to think of the right thing to say. "That's something I don't know, but I can tell you how I feel if you want me to."

"I do."

"I hope it gets better, but if it doesn't, I really believe you'll find ways to offset what's wrong. I think people can build up their strong points enough to compensate for their weaker ones."

That made sense, but I still felt clumsy when I couldn't walk a straight line. In school I was afraid I'd topple over if I got jostled on the stairs. Escalators were something I avoided, and I had to put my arms out to my sides if I tried to walk down even the most gentle slope.

"Do you mean that I'll be less of a Godzilla as time goes by?"

Looking a bit stern, Jack took both my hands in his and said, "Gustie, you're not a bumbling monster. No way. You're still sort of learning what you can and can't do. If you want to compare yourself to an animal, try . . . oh . . . Bambi."

"Bambi? Why Bambi?"

"Bambi had to get used to those long, untested legs and sometimes went sprawling. Even if your balance is never as good as it once was, you'll be more sure-footed, I think, after you get used to what you can and can't expect of yourself."

His blue eyes deepened a shade as he looked at me, and the effect was like a shot of courage labeled, "You're going to be fine." Then he dropped my hands, stood up, and reached out for my arm. "Come on, little deer, let's go back to the car and wipe out that picnic basket."

Still sitting there on the breakwater, I felt myself melting. "Thanks, Jack," I said as I let him pull me up.

We spread a blanket out on the warm sand. The wind was refreshing without being too chilly. We made small talk as we ate; it still amazed me how well I could read Jack's lips. About halfway through our meal, Jack got sort of down. I could tell by the way he was looking out at the water and not saying much. Then, before I could ask what was wrong, he volunteered.

"I got a letter from my dad, yesterday. A couple of months ago he promised me some money for a used car. Now he says he's changed his mind.

"It's not even the car so much, Gustie. I mean, I'm not denying that I'd like my own car. Who wouldn't? But Dad built me up, talking about different models and their features, and I got used to the idea of having my own car this summer and for school next fall. He'd convinced me he'd follow through this time."

I didn't like people backing out of promises any more than Jack did. I could imagine how let down he felt. Then I picked up on his last sentence.

"This time? You mean there were others?"

"Yeah," he said, pulling his knees up to his chin. He tried to talk with his chin on his knees, but it changed the way his mouth looked so much that I couldn't understand him.

"I didn't get that last part," I told him.

"Oh," he said, suddenly understanding why I'd had the difficulty, "I just said that Dad has done stuff like this before."

He stopped talking then, and for a minute I thought that he didn't want to say anything more. But he did.

"What's always hurt me is Dad's empty promising. Why does he promise so much when most times I never even ask for anything? One time he took me shopping and promised me an elaborate train set, complete with miniature mountains and villages. Gustie, he talked about it every single night for two weeks before my tenth birthday. By my birthday, naturally I really did want that train set."

I could picture Jack as a ten-year-old, expectation dancing in those bright blue eyes.

"And?" I coaxed.

"He gave me a ship model to build and added that he'd just bought season tickets for himself and *Larry* to the St. Louis Cards' home games. The funny thing is that I would have been perfectly satisfied with the ship if he hadn't plugged the train set so hard every single day.

"Don't get me wrong when I say this. I love my brother, but Dad used to shower Larry with stuff—the best bike, professional sports equipment, a car. I never was upset because of that. Larry's nine years older than I am, so we never wanted the same things at the same time."

Jack shook his head in disbelief. I could see his disappointment in not getting the promised train all those years ago. I wondered why a father would act like that, and I had no answer. Money hadn't seemed to be the reason; his dad had bought all those expensive things for Larry.

Reaching out to put my hand over his, I said, "Oh, Jack, I'm really sorry."

"It's okay. The odd thing is that I never resented any of Dad's lavish surprises for Larry. Larry's great."

Jack had perked up at his own mention of his older brother, so I took the cue, stood up to stretch, and changed the subject from broken promises to Larry.

"How did Larry get through school using just sign language?" I asked. I couldn't imagine some little kid learning how to write or add without understanding the teacher.

Jack was more like himself again as he said, "You're probably thinking of school as in public school. Larry went to a special school, Gustie, a residential school expressly for deaf students."

"Did you say residential? Do you mean he had to live there?" The idea made me think of some awful kind of building I'd seen in old movies on TV, all dark and spidery and where there was no laughter. "*Poor Larry*," I thought.

Almost as if Jack had read my mind, he said, "You're feeling sorry for him, aren't you, because he went to a special school?"

"Shouldn't I? It sounds so terrible to shut a little boy away there."

Jack, from his expression, gave a strange little laugh and shook his head. "Boy, you've got some picture, haven't you? It wasn't terrible at all. It was a place where he had friends who also had hearing losses and where the teachers and staff knew sign language and had been trained in the use of special teaching methods."

"*Scratch the spiders*," I thought, But it still seemed cruel to separate a child from his parents. I thought of Mom flipping pancakes before school while Dad and I drank our juice and kidded around, and Dad helping me with my science project in sixth grade. We were a family seven days a week.

"Did your parents ever get to see him?" I asked.

"Of course. We lived about 100 miles from the school, so Larry could come home every weekend if he wanted to, and of course he was home for holidays and summers. Larry was always glad to come home, but he also was eager to go back to school. It was his turf, Gustie, where he could communicate effortlessly and just be a boy learning in a way and at a rate of speed that took his deafness into consideration. He didn't have to keep up with the hearing kids. Living at home might have isolated him from friends. Remember that Larry didn't talk, like you do; and he wasn't able to speechread his friends."

"Oh, that's right."

"He lived in a red brick building," Jack continued, "that looked a lot like a college dorm. In fact, the entire school, which included several buildings, a laundry, and physical plant, looked like a college campus, not the Frankenstein setting you thought of when I said *residential*."

I felt embarrassed that I'd jumped to the wrong conclusion, and again, Jack sensed my mood.

He said, "Oh, come on, you don't have to be embarrassed with me." He put a hand around each of my arms and held me at arm's length. I could tell by the gentleness in his eyes that I really didn't have to feel embarrassed. He wasn't just trying to make me feel better. He really understood my reaction.

I smiled and let him pull me close for a hug. Then we continued our discussion.

"It's weird," I said. "I'm still thinking of Larry with his sign language and special school. Jack, I feel sometimes as if I'm deaf and yet not deaf. Does that sound crazy?"

"No. Tell me more."

"I can't imagine myself in a residential school, and I'm as deaf as a post. I can't imagine myself using sign language all the time. I mean, look at us today. I've understood practically every word you've said. I feel so comfortable. I like words. I'm even getting used to watching people and imagining their voices as they talk to me."

"I know," Jack said, "but Larry didn't have your advantage of normal hearing to develop a comfortableness with words. Your culture depended upon speech and hearing. It was always oral—*o-r-a-l*—and aural—*a-u-r-a-l*," he explained, differentiating between the two similar-looking words by spelling them out for me, "while Larry's was not. It just underlines my belief that deaf people aren't all alike."

A year ago, I wouldn't have thought of my culture as being oral and aural. I wondered if most people give it a thought unless something happens to mess up the speech-hearing flow of words.

It meant a lot to me that Jack didn't lump all hearing impaired people together. I smiled at him and said, "I'm glad you feel that way."

"Me too," he answered with a grin. Then he got serious again and said, "Even though I agree that sign language probably isn't for you, at least not in the way it is for Larry, I'd like to show you something."

He began to make interesting shapes with his right hand.

"What's that?"

"It's called fingerspelling. There's an alphabet made with the fingers of one hand. They're symbols just as A, B, and C are written symbols for the components that make written words. In fingerspelling, you spell out a word letter-by-letter with those hand symbols. You know how I just spelled out *oral* and *aural*?"

He waited for my nod and then said, "Well, I might have fingerspelled them instead. Watch."

It was amazing. I watched his right hand make an O. It even looked like an O, with all the fingers meeting at the thumb. Then he crossed his middle finger and his index finger like people do when they're crossing their fingers for good luck. Then he made a fist, only with his thumb standing straight up. Finally, he made what I could tell was an L with his thumb and index finger and the rest of his fingers tucked into his palm.

"Oral?"

He patted me on the back.

"Hey, that was neat. I could tell the O and the L without even knowing the fingerspelling alphabet, They looked so much like when you write them."

"The other two were the R," he told me, making the crossed-fingers symbol again, "and the A," he added as he formed the one that looked like a variation on a fist.

"Do you want to learn the alphabet? It's not very hard."

I said I did, and for the next several minutes we practiced five letters at a time until I remembered them. Then we moved on to the next five, practicing those and the earlier ones I'd learned, and on down the alphabet.

"We'll keep practicing until you can zip right through all twenty-six letters," Jack said.

"You're a good teacher," I told him. "When do people use fingerspelling? How useful is it?"

" I guess only the person using it can say. It is for Larry. American

Sign Language has signs for whole concepts and ideas and goes much faster than if each word is fingerspelled. But signers know how to fingerspell and they use it to express concepts that don't have signs, like most proper nouns."

"Names are sometimes a problem for me, too," I told Jack, thinking about how I'd been introduced recently to a neighbor's visiting niece. When I didn't get the name the first time Mrs. Toppins told it to me, she repeated it, but as hard as I tried, it still came out: "I'd like you to meet my niece, *Mushy Mush*." I'd finally just given up and thought of her as "the niece" all weekend.

"That's why I thought of showing you fingerspelling. If you and I are together and we meet someone for the first time, I could just do a little finger magic and—*voila*—you'd get the person's name."

"That'd be neat."

"I'd like you to meet," he said, beginning to fingerspell *S-a-n-t-a C-l-a-u-s*.

"Santa Claus!" I told him, pleased to have been able to decipher the fingerspelled name.

"How about_____." He spelled some impossible long name, going extremely fast. It didn't bother me because I could tell he was teasing me.

"How about a *k-i-s-s*," he fingerspelled.

Middle Ground

•

I continued to see Jack and Lenore almost every day. They seemed to really like each other, which I thought they would. Not only were they both nice people to start with, but each of my new friends seemed very accepting of my hearing loss. I didn't feel self-conscious with either of them. I just *was*, if you know what I mean. I was just Gustie, not The Deaf Girl.

Although Lenore didn't know it yet, Jack and I were even working on setting up a blind date for her with one of Jack's friends. I thought it would be neat to double.

School was going okay lately. Nobody had heard from Sara since her accident, which worried me a little. It had been five weeks already. Lenore told me that before the accident Sara had been acting different and nasty to other people besides me. One day, when Lenore was trying out for girls' choir, she had seen Sara yelling at Dana in front of everyone at tryouts because Dana had beaten her out.

My mom kept in touch with Sara's mom, so we knew that Sara's progress was slow. Mrs. Marler didn't give out details, but she did say that Sara had some emotional problems that had to be worked out. At least that helped explain Sara's weird behavior over the last ten months. I still hoped we could be friends again, so I was happy that she was getting help to get better.

Jack kept suggesting that I meet his brother and sister-in-law. I wasn't sure about that because I didn't know what to expect. They were both deaf, and so was I, but they used sign language and I talked. I just wasn't sure how it would go. Jack told me not to worry, that everything would be fine; so after about ten days, I agreed to go.

Before we went over to Larry and Pam's, Jack gave me some suggestions about how to act with them.

"When you speak to Pam and Larry, talk directly to them, just like they could hear you," Jack advised. "I'll interpret everything you say into sign language, but look at them, not me, when you have something to say to them. It's kind of an unwritten interpreting etiquette. Do you know what I mean?"

Even though their situation was different from mine, I thought I knew. I remembered people who hadn't talked directly to me even though we were in the same room. They'd say to my parents, "Tell Gustie_____" or "Does Gustie like_____?" Sometimes I felt invisible.

"I think so," I told him. "Instead of saying to you, 'Jack, please tell Pam and Larry I like their house,' I should look at them and say, 'I like your house.'"

Jack looked pleased, nodding that I had the right idea.

As we pulled to a stop in front of a small but brightly painted split-level, Jack said, "Here we are. Don't be nervous."

My hands were sweaty, though. I knew that Pam and Larry would just be people, but I was afraid that they might not like me because I didn't sign. I didn't want them to think I was a snob because I could talk and speechread, and I didn't want to do anything embarrassing, like forget to talk straight to them.

A narrow flagstone path wound toward the front door, and I noticed how well kept their yard was. On the tiny porch, Jack gently poked an elbow into my side to get my attention and said, "You'll do fine, Gustie. They're going to love you; anyway, they're pretty special people themselves."

As Jack knocked, I wondered how they'd know we were there, but there wasn't time to ask him before a man who looked like an older

Jack answered the door. He had Jack's coloring, with those same blue eyes and black hair. He was a dream. Standing at his side was a petite, brown-haired woman.

Larry said something in sign language, his fingers flying, and motioned for us to come in. Then he led us into the living room.

When Jack introduced us, I fingerspelled, "Hi." I was glad that Jack had taught me how to do it. I also said, "Pam and Larry, it's nice to meet you. Jack has told me a lot about you."

Jack told them this in sign language, and Larry and Pam both smiled. Larry signed something. Even though I didn't understand the signs, I felt his warmth in his facial expression. Meanwhile, Pam fingerspelled for my benefit, no doubt, "Hi, Gustie," before sitting down.

We made small talk just like anybody else would about the weather, school, and their cozy home.

Then I noticed a beautiful painting over the fireplace. I couldn't stop staring at it. It was a watercolor of a unicorn wearing a garland of flowers. Whoever had painted it was a wonderful artist. When I drew my stare back to the people in the room, Pam and Larry were watching me.

"I was admiring that painting. I really like it," I said, making eye contact with Pam, who seemed to be able to watch both Jack's signing and my expressions at the same time. "I don't think I've ever seen a better unicorn."

"That's saying a lot," Jack explained. "Gustie has a thing about unicorns; she always notices posters and paintings of them in stores."

Pam smiled, and when she did, her whole face lit up.

Larry started signing something very rapidly. He was grinning. I looked back and forth from him to Jack, whose lips I read, and finally back at Pam.

"You mean Pam painted the unicorn?"

"And that's not all," Jack told me, also signing for their benefit. Then he signed something to Larry that he didn't interpret for me. It felt like there was something they didn't want me to know. They had matching expressions that reminded me of two little boys with a secret they were finally going to share with me.

At this point, Larry got up and walked over to a wide bookcase, took out a slim book, and brought it back to Jack. Larry looked proud, but Pam was actually blushing. She shrugged in a gesture that seemed to mean, "Larry's impossible sometimes, but I love him." I'd seen that look before on Mom's face.

I was totally confused by what was going on. Then Jack touched my arm and held the book up to get my attention. Slowly, he turned it over so that I could see the front of the book's dust jacket.

To my surprise, I saw Pam's painting—the one right over the fireplace—on the cover of a well-known children's book.

"No wonder you look so proud," I told Larry. Then I said to Pam, "This is wonderful, Pam. I had no idea."

We talked about the book for a while, and then Pam autographed it for me to take home.

What had I expected, anyway, when I met these people? It wasn't this beautiful house or a professional book illustrator. It didn't make me feel good to admit to myself, but I realized that I had stereotyped Pam and Larry. I had expected them to be inferior somehow. Now I saw how unfair that was.

Pam got my attention and said, through Jack's interpretation, "Gustie, it's show-and-tell time now." When she got up, we all followed her through the living room. "Come on. You won't believe some of the gadgets we've got. You might not have any use for some of them, but it's nice to know they're there if you want them."

First, we saw a small typewriter-like machine on a table next to the telephone and a lamp.

"This is called a TTY or TDD," Jack told me. "TTY is the older name. It stands for teletypewriter, and that's what the machine used to look like. Now most TTYs are small like this one; some people call them TDDs, which stands for telecommunications device for the deaf. No matter what size the machine is, though, almost everybody who has one calls it a TTY.

"The TTY lets deaf people use the telephone. When the phone rings, the light flashes, so Pam and Larry know someone is calling. To answer, they put the phone receiver into the TTY cradle. They type a short message, which somehow is converted into tonal bleeps. Then the bleeps are changed back into alphabet letters that appear on the caller's TTY screen. Watch, Larry will show you how it works."

Larry sat down, flipped a switch on the machine, and began typing. As he typed I saw alphabet letters march across the long, narrow screen in bright green computer-type print: HI GUSTIE. THIS IS LARRY. HOW ARE YOU? GA.

I was sure my mouth dropped open as I watched the words move across the screen. "This is great," I said. "I've never seen anything like it. What does GA mean?"

"It stands for *go ahead*," Jack said. "It means that you've finished your message and it's the other person's turn to talk through typing."

Just then Larry motioned for me to take his place in the chair.

"Oh, no," I started to protest. I was afraid I'd goof it up. I knew the machine must be expensive, and I didn't even know how to type on a regular typewriter.

"Come on," urged Jack. "You can't break it."

"*Here goes*," I thought.

Picking out the keys one by one, I typed: HI PAM AND LARRY. THIS IS A NEAT MACHINE.

"It seems like magic," I told them. I didn't really understand how the TTY worked, but the idea of using a phone again sent shivers through me.

"Mother always calls it the miracle machine," Jack said. "These machines are almost constantly being made better. Right now, most of them work only if there's a TTY at both ends of the call, but I think it won't be long until they can be used with any regular phone."

"Who do you talk to on it?" I asked them.

"My parents have one, so does Larry's mom," Pam explained. "We have deaf friends who have them, and now everything from insurance companies to take-out pizza places are getting them. It's also a relief to know that we can call the fire department or an ambulance on the TTY."

Larry signed something to Jack and Jack said, "They have a code with the emergency services. Typing on a TTY takes longer than speaking the same message on the regular phone. Pam and Larry can just type 'Code Twelve—fire,' and the dispatcher will match their number—twelve—to a list that gives their names and this address."

"It really is a miracle machine," I said appreciatively.

But the TTY was only the beginning. Pam and Larry took me around their home and showed me their other "gadgets," as Pam called them.

The next gadget was the captioned TV.

"Do you mean that TV shows on your set have writing with the picture to tell what's being said?" I asked. "Boy, would that be nice. Some shows are so hard to follow. Often I can follow the plot, but getting what the actors say is very hard, and I miss a lot."

Larry nodded and then explained in signs, "Not all shows are captioned yet, but we get a good cross-section of what's on TV. In the past couple of weeks, for example, there's been a closed-captioned James Bond movie, situation comedies, the evening news, and first-rate programs on PBS. Pam never misses 'Masterpiece Theatre.'"

"Why is it called *closed* captioning?"

Jack said, "Only those TV sets with an adapter or decoder let the viewer see the captions. People watching the same show without an adapter don't see the printing."

"I see," I told him, wondering if some of my favorite programs from when I could hear were closed-captioned.

"Let me see if I can find a captioned show for you," Pam said, turning on the set and flipping the dial. She stopped when she came to a channel with black boxes along the bottom of the screen. Inside the boxes were the captions, in white. They were very easy to read.

It was a program about iron bridges. The narrator was off-camera, so without the captions, anyone who couldn't hear wouldn't have know what he was saying. The camera showed beautiful scenes of the

English countryside, and the writing along the bottom of the T screen identified the areas and told the history of iron bridges. I'd never been big on bridges, but to me, it seemed like the most marvelous show I'd ever seen. I got goose bumps because I was so happy I wasn't closed out.

After staring at the set for some time, I looked at my friends again and said, "This is just wonderful. I feel sort of choked up. I've missed TV."

"They understand," Jack assured me.

Pam signed that she had also been amazed at first. She told me to come back any time and watch TV with her. Larry seconded the invitation.

Before Jack and I left their house, Pam and Larry also showed me their door light signal, light-up alarm clock, and smoke detector, and something that seemed as new to Jack as it was to me.

"What's that?" Jack asked, pointing to a little black box with a cord attached to it.

Pam's cheeks turned pink. Larry beamed.

"We'll be needing it in about seven months," Larry told us. "It's a baby cry alarm. A light will flash to let us know when our baby cries.

Jack was as surprised as I was. He gave Pam a kiss and his brother a bear hug.

"That's wonderful," I told them.

Everyone was smiling as we left.

"I'm so glad I went," I told Jack as we drove back to my house. "Thanks for taking me. They're so friendly and warm, so . . . so . . ."

"Normal?" Jack supplied.

I nodded.

Meeting Pam and Larry made such a big impression on me that I decided I was ready to meet some of Mr. Tate's hearing-impaired students. He had suggested it several weeks ago, but I wasn't ready then.

On the day I visited the group, Mr. Tate met me before class in a very large room that was separated into smaller sections by movable walls.

"Several classes can be held at the same time this way," he explained. "These partitions move easily, allowing us to change the sizes of the individual classrooms. You'll probably find most special education classes small in comparison to yours."

The classroom he led me to had a dozen chairs arranged in a semi-circle that faced a chalkboard.

"You can use the visitor's chair," he told me, pointing to a chair that was just to the side of the semi-circle. The furniture arrangement allowed each student to see everybody in the class.

Before we had time to talk more, the students began coming into the room. I counted six girls and five guys. They looked just like other students in my school, except that many of them wore hearing aids. Most of them came into the room in little clots of twos and threes. They were signing back and forth to one another. Their communication looked strange and yet familiar. I wondered if the signing was about the same things hearing kids talked about just before class.

I realized I was twisting my amethyst ring on my finger. I was nervous. I wanted them to like me and I also wanted to like them.

Mr. Tate must have noticed my ring-twisting because he said, "Everything will be fine. Just observe them today, Gustie, and we'll talk about your perceptions later."

"Okay," I told him.

It took them a while to get settled into their chairs, but when they were, most of them noticed me. I wondered if they were signing, "Who's she?"

"Class, I'd like you to meet Gustie Blaine," Mr. Tate told them as I smiled my best smile at them. I felt like a bug under a microscope. It's not that they were unfriendly. They were just all staring at me. My ring made another full circle around my finger.

"Gustie is deaf," he continued. "She has not been deaf all her life. She had meningitis last summer, and now she cannot hear anything, even with a hearing aid." Several students looked sad as he said that part. "She's doing very well in regular classes, but she wanted to meet you and see what our classes are like."

Several students started signing among themselves, and three of them pointed to themselves. I had no idea what they were saying, but they looked so enthusiastic that I wished I knew.

Mr. Tate explained what was going on. "Gustie, the three pointers had meningitis, just like you did, only at a much younger age. The others were born with serious hearing impairments or had other illnesses at early ages."

There was more signing within the semi-circle.

"They want to know if you can sign."

Remembering Jack's advice to speak directly to a signer, I made eye contact with them as Mr. Tate interpreted my words into signs. "I'm sorry, but I don't sign. I can fingerspell, though," I added.

Making the individual alphabet letters one-by-one with the fingers of my right hand, I spelled out, "Hi, I'm glad to be here."

They returned my greeting in fingerspelling. Then Mr. Tate got down to business and began class.

Despite the signing and hearing aids, they looked like any other class. Some of them, for example, were paying more attention than others. Two or three of them were writing either secret notes or other assignments that probably were due later that day. They tried to write when they thought Mr. Tate wasn't looking. How many times had I seen that in a regular classroom? I'd even done it myself.

Two girls were signing back and forth in a way that looked private, as though it wasn't meant to be read by anyone else. What were they confiding? It was probably something about boys, just as it usually was in a regular classroom.

At one point when Mr. Tate had his back to the class, a wad of paper hit me on the cheek, and the class giggled. Again, I compared. I couldn't count all the spitballs that had flown across the classrooms I'd been in.

These students didn't seem that different from hearing students. They were discussing an English assignment from a book on famous Americans. The class had read a chapter yesterday, and today they were going over workbook exercises on the chapter.

That's when I noticed the difference from hearing students. The text of the chapter was on a much easier reading level than I was used to. The workbook exercises reminded me of fourth grade, even though the students were my age or a little older. Mr. Tate seemed very concerned with how much they had understood of what they'd read.

Several students had papers that weren't finished.

"Bring them in tomorrow for sure," Mr. Tate told them as he signed to them. There was a certain no-nonsense expression on his face that suggested a stern voice.

"They are protesting that it was a hard, long assignment," he explained to me.

And it looked so short and easy! I frowned. My feelings were confused. How could they be so different and yet not that different from hearing students? Where did I fit in? I was hearing impaired just as they were, and yet I was also very different. I knew right then that I did not belong in their special education classes as more than a visitor.

"What did you think of the class, Gustie?" Mr. Tate asked when I met him in his office after school.

I wasn't sure what to say. I wanted to be honest, but I didn't know how to describe my mixed feelings. Wasn't I supposed to magically fit in with other deaf people because I was deaf too? With Jack along, I had seemed to fit in with Pam and Larry, but the classroom situation was different. How could I explain to Mr. Tate that I felt less a part of his class than of hearing classes?

"I'm glad I went," I began, "but I felt that I didn't belong there as more than an observer. I don't think it was just because they sign and I don't."

When I paused, he encouraged me to go on with a nod of his head, as though he agreed with me.

"Honestly, Mr. Tate, I'm not trying to judge them unfairly. It's not that I think I'm any better than they are."

"I didn't think you were. You seemed to be there with an open mind."

"I think I was. It's just that, is there any rule that says I belong with the deaf just because I'm deaf? I feel closer to Lenore all the time and she hears normally. Jack, my boyfriend, also hears normally. I'm even feeling better again in school now that I have good notes. How could I trade translating Latin or reading Chaucer for fourth-grade biographies?

"It's not that I don't respect those students in your class. I don't feel any better than they are because I can do school work they can't. My boyfriend, who has a deaf brother, has even gotten me over my fear of learning sign language. I thought it was beautiful to see your class signing and talking back and forth with that language. But they also seem to be cut off from the rest of the school. I don't want to be like that, Mr. Tate.

"I'm deaf and yet not deaf. I am deaf physically, but inside, way deep inside, I'm still the me I've always been. I can't erase all those years when I could hear normally. Where do I fit in?"

I was searching for more to say, but Mr. Tate broke in. "You are right in the middle, Gustie."

"The middle?"

"Yes. It's a tough spot to be in. The students you saw today are language handicapped in a way you are not. Their native language is American Sign Language, not English. You can't just learn a bunch of signs and automatically fit in. Their experiences, learning, and frames of reference are different than yours.

"You've told me that you loved music. I'll use that as a touchstone. There *is* music for them, but it's not a hearing person's idea of music. My students perceive music in terms of vibrations they feel or as occasional loud beats they hear. You, on the other hand, think of music in terms of intricate blendings of sound. You know how the scales go and how French horns and violins sound. Your frame of reference, because you once heard normally and studied music, is different.

"I believe this difference extends to many cultural and educational aspects, Gustie. The answer is not to give up your conception of music just because you are deaf now, and it is not to give up speaking English or reading what you like just because you are deaf now. Do you know what I'm getting at?"

I wasn't sure, but I was willing to voice my guess. "You're saying that I have to identify my own frames of reference and learn to be comfortable with them?"

His smile warmed his gray eyes as he said, "Yes."

As I lay in bed that night, it suddenly came to me. I knew what belonging was. I had been right in Mr. Tate's office about needing to find my own frames of reference and learning to be comfortable with them.

Belonging was looking into yourself and finding out who you really were. It was finding out what was important to you and what made you feel good about yourself.

Handicapped, disabled, crippled, deaf as a post—maybe how others felt didn't really matter. I had to be true to myself and like myself no matter what other people thought or said. I realized that mistaken attitudes and intolerance are greater handicaps than the more obvious ones, like deafness.

Middle ground. That's where I was. I had felt stuck in some no man's land halfway between deafness and hearing, but now I saw that being on middle ground didn't just limit me. It also gave me choices.

I thought of friendships and realized that I might feel comfortable with some deaf people and not others, just as I was choosy in my friendships with hearing people. I was free to decide who I wanted as my friend.

I thought about my future. Mr. Tate had shown me a book on the lives of deaf people. To my surprise, there had been a wide variety of careers, ranging from law to sports to teaching. Middle ground gave me options about a career. I might even work for some kind of advanced college degree.

The changes deafness brought did not have to ruin my life. I belonged on this earth, and I was still free to be me.

Putting It Into Words

•

I wanted very much to share my new feelings with my parents. I wanted to let them know that I had choices in communicating and that I had options in life. I wanted more than anything else to change their hope from the hope of restored hearing, which only led to disappointment and frustration now that it was unrealistic, to the hope of coping and making the best of things.

With this in mind, I walked into the kitchen one day after school. Mom was paring apples for a pie, and there was something reassuring about the floury kitchen counter. It's not that I believe a woman's place is in the home, but Mom's being there made me think of how safe and protected I felt when I was a little girl.

I set my books on an unfloured counter and made small talk until just after Mom had placed the pie into the oven.

"Mom, can I tell you something really personal?" I asked as she sat down with a mug of coffee.

"Of course you can, darling," she said, giving me a reassuring look.

"Well, I've been doing a lot of thinking," I began. "Maybe speech-reading isn't the only way to go. I mean, I've got all that stuff learned pretty well by now, and I still miss words here and there, even with you. It's a lot worse with people I don't know, or even with Dad. His lips are so thin. It . . . "

"I know how hard it must be, Gustie, but you are making such excellent progress. Please try not to get discouraged, honey. All the experts who have seen you tell me that you are an outstanding lipreader. You should feel very proud. Your dad and I are."

Was she going to set up another wall? Why couldn't we talk about this topic? Mom and Dad were very patient about repeating words for me. We did communicate about many things. Where my hearing loss was concerned, though, Mom and Dad still had a strained look that shut me out. I wondered if they talked about my deafness when they were alone. I guess they did, at least some of the time, but didn't I have any right to be part of some of those discussions? I thought so.

Somehow I had to get through to Mom. "But Mom, that's just the point. I'm supposed to be an *outstanding* speechreader. I'm happy I'm good at it, but don't you see that even for an outstanding speechreader there are limits? It would help me so much if you knew how to finger-spell. Mom . . . "

"Augusta, you already know how your father and I feel about sign language. It would rob you of your speech and set you back so far."

"You are wrong, Mom," I shouted, getting up from my chair. "You are wrong! I wasn't even talking about sign language. Fingerspelling is just alphabet letters made with your fingers. If we all knew . . . "

"Please. No more, Gustie. Speech and lipreading are the only way to go."

Talk about closed minds! I was so furious and frustrated. Who did she think she was, managing my life and picking *her* favorite communication option? She didn't know what it was like to be deaf. It wasn't her ears. It wasn't her life.

I wanted to shake her, but as calmly as I could, I said, "If you ever open your mind enough, you can let me finish what I was trying to say, or go see Mr. Tate at my school."

Then I turned my back to her and ran up the stairs to Jasmine. My cat didn't give a hoot whether I communicated in words, in signs, or by standing on my head and wiggling my toes. Jasmine loved and accepted me without strings.

I understood some of my parents' fears about sign language. I'd had them, too, and still had some, in fact.

That part didn't upset me. What bothered me was that somewhere along the line, my parents had slammed the door on that option without even talking to me about it. Maybe somebody at one of the doctors' offices turned them against sign language. I just didn't know.

What got me was that we couldn't sit down and talk about anything to do with my hearing loss.

What other options had they flatly rejected? I'm sure they thought they had all the best choices in mind for me, but did they have all the facts? Did they really understand how hard it is to be deaf in a hearing world? I had to live with myself twenty-four hours a day and I felt I had the right to make most of the decisions myself, or at least be involved in making them.

What could I do to get my feelings across to them? Each time I tried, I got cut off. For all I knew, Mom thought I was trying to tell her that I was going to stop talking forever, like some monk on permanent retreat, and use only signs for the rest of my life. She never even let me finish.

I needed to let both my parents know how I felt, not just about communicating but also about the whole deafness thing and their attitudes. Since I couldn't talk to them about it, I decided to write them a letter. I hated to write letters, but it seemed the only thing to do.

It took me all afternoon. I had a hard time at first, but once I began, the words kept flowing.

Dear Mom and Dad,

Sixteen is sort of a milestone birthday. I know I've changed a lot since my fifteenth birthday, and I want to share my feelings with you because I love you both very much, and I know you love me.

It's pretty hard to imagine myself as a parent and having my child get meningitis and lose her hearing. I know it hasn't been easy for you. I'm grateful for all you did to see that I had the best doctors. We all kept hoping I'd get back to normal and be the old me with good hearing. It just didn't happen, though, and no amount of wishful thinking is going to bring back what's gone.

You asked me what I wanted for my sixteenth birthday. I want us to stop kidding ourselves that I'm still a hearing person with just a little hearing problem. I want to be loved and respected as the best deaf me I can be, not as a mock hearing person. I have no room to grow if people expect me to be what I no longer am.

I'm still me, Mom and Dad, but I have some new, very different needs than I had before.

I'm glad that I know the basics of speechreading. I love to talk, and I get a certain joy in speechreading well. Speechreading is a limited art, though, and I think I owe it to myself to consider all the communication options available to me.

I don't think I'd be happy using sign language all the time, but if I learn some and use it with a deaf friend, it's not automatically going to make me forget how to talk or speechread. Sign language isn't second-rate English; it's a beautiful language of its own. The people you see using it who do not talk have not had my advantage of fifteen years of normal hearing. They don't have all my communication options, but that doesn't make them or their language inferior. It isn't a measure of intelligence.

As for fingerspelling, it could be a great timesaver. It would also free me from the enormous strain of trying to speechread a person's name or getting a word that looks impossible on the lips. Think of fingerspelling as an easy, quick clarification. It's not that different from writing a name on paper, but it's faster and more convenient.

All I want is to use all the resources available to me in communicating. Why should I reject this or that method and make life harder than it needs to be?

I'm learning that I still have options in life. Sure, I may face discrimination and personal limitations, but I'd rather try at something and fail than never try at all. I know that failure is only relative. As long as I don't fail myself and my own expectations, I won't consider myself a failure or handicapped, no matter how others judge me. I don't want to be hidden away from responsibility or sheltered from making decisions for myself.

You probably have been wondering what deaf people can do for a living. Well, I've found out that they can do almost everything. There are deaf teachers, lawyers, dentists, writers, hospital workers—the list is endless, Mom and Dad, so don't worry about my finding something. At sixteen, most of my hearing friends haven't made up their minds about a career either.

Deaf people marry (and not necessarily other deaf people), have children, drive cars, and do just about anything hearing people do except hear. I couldn't be deaf at a better point in history. There are special telephones, baby cry light signals, and closed-captioned television. Technology will be opening new doors all the time.

I don't think acceptance of any big change in life necessarily lands in a person's lap. It doesn't come all at once. Truthfully, I doubt if I'll ever accept being deaf 100%. Maybe people who are born deaf do, but I'll always know what I'm missing. Sometimes I may long to hear a song I used to love or use a regular phone or hear someone's voice. Acceptance is something I'll work on day by day.

I really believe that my life doesn't have to be less good than it might have been. I want you to believe that, too, and accept my hearing loss along with me. Let's talk about it when we need to. Please joke with me again. Please scold me like you used to when my room is mess. As Gram would say, let's stop pussyfooting around and just act like the loving family we really are.

"Well, Jasmine," I told my cat as she looked at me sleepily, "that does it. I don't know if they'll kiss me or kill me when they read this."

Then I signed my name.

What I didn't expect was for them to do nothing about my letter. I wondered if they were mad at me. Maybe they thought my ideas were too bossy and uncompromising. Maybe they were disappointed in me for writing the letter.

They didn't seem angry or disappointed, though. In fact, Mom and Dad were smiling at me more than usual—real smiles, too, not the fakey ones. The strained look that had been on their faces ever since I had lost my hearing seemed almost gone. I couldn't explain the way they looked at each other, but their secretive smiles reminded me of the way they looked the year they surprised me with a family trip to

Disney World.

I guessed it all had to do with my upcoming birthday. I'd sort of hinted for a nice quartz watch. Mom was a jewelry nut, and she got very excited when she gave somebody something special.

I stretched lazily in bed the morning of my sixteenth birthday. It was a sunny Friday, and a shaft of sunlight made my bed a toasty little nest.

Lying there, I realized that I no longer dreaded waking up and doing my secret voice test to find out if I could hear anything that day. I knew I wouldn't. I didn't know if I'd ever really get used to being deaf, but the endless silence no longer seemed like a Greek tragedy, either. In a way, it was even a relief not to be a human yo-yo with a percentage of hearing to measure my days into "good" and "bad."

Some people thought deafness automatically made a person's eyes sharper. I knew this wasn't true. I still needed my contact lenses. There were no supernatural visitations or anything like that. But I did see life differently than I used to. I appreciated the little things more.

A rainy day now brought beautiful cloud formations, not just inconvenience, dampness, and canceled plans. A lone flower growing defiantly through a crack in the sidewalk seemed that much prettier to me because of the emotions, like loneliness, I'd felt since my illness.

Human kindness seemed that much warmer in contrast to discrimination and lack of understanding. I had a new sense of the worth of a simple smile or the words "I understand."

I realized I'd taken human beings pretty much for granted. I'd never stopped to appreciate how adaptable we are. Now I knew that if a part of the body failed, a person could usually find a way to make up for it. Speechreading and sign language were perfect examples of backup systems a person could use in case the hearing mechanism didn't work right. In the same way, each person has a certain freedom of attitude, no matter how rough the situation.

I realized that as a hearing person, I had been missing some things in life because I'd been too busy going places, doing things, and trying to be popular.

Just then, Jasmine broke my train of thought as she jumped, purring, onto my bed. I loved the feel of her purr.

"Wow, Jas," I told her, "I think this birthday is going to my head." I felt strangely content as I said it.

At school that day, Lenore surprised me with a crepe paper and balloon decorated locker. She also gave me a French edition of *The Little Prince*. "In French," she told me, "because of your unswerving desire to master the language in spite of Monsieur Armour." She also produced a small birthday cake at lunchtime, which we shared with everyone sitting near our table.

Jack didn't have the same lunch hour that we had. He and I were going to a movie after my birthday dinner at home.

Mom made my favorite dinner that night—homemade lasagna and a salad. When we had finished eating, Dad handed me a package and said, "Happy birthday, sweet sixteen."

The package he handed me was long and narrow—much too large and heavy to be a quartz watch. I didn't really need a watch; I still had my old Timex.

"Thanks, Mom and Dad," I told them, wondering what it could be.

Mom always wrapped presents so beautifully that opening one seemed like destroying a work of art. This one was wrapped with pale blue paper that had brightly colored rainbows on it and a ribbon the color of sunshine. I tried to think of any prebirthday hints I'd dropped, but the package had me completely stumped.

I laid it on the table and turned it slowly as I untaped the edges of the wrapping paper. Finally, it peeled away. I saw some writing on a brown cardboard box, and my heart gave a quick little thump. Could it be what I thought it was? I turned the box over.

It was!

"A closed-caption decoder! Oh, Mom and Dad, thank you," I said, getting up to kiss each of them. Dad helped me pull the sturdy staples out of the box. "I don't believe it!"

And I really didn't believe it. After my visit with Pam and Larry, I'd tried to tell my parents about all the gadgets available to make life easier and more enjoyable for deaf people. They didn't want any part of it, as though accepting a special signal or gadget was giving in to the enemy, my deafness. Their attitude was sort of like, if Gustie doesn't use sign language or use any special gadgets, she's still our same little girl—still normal. I guessed it was part of the grieving process that Jack had told me about.

But now here was something made just for deaf people. I didn't try to hide the puddles in my eyes.

"Your letter was just beautiful, Gustie," Mom said, "and it really opened our eyes."

"We'll cherish it forever," Dad added.

"I was afraid you'd be mad at me. I sort of let you have it."

"It's just what we needed, honey," Dad assured me. "We aren't mad at you. In fact, we owe you an apology."

Nodding, Mom added, "We felt that we were protecting you from hurt and disappointment. We didn't realize how we were shutting you out. Do you remember the day we sat at the kitchen table and you tried to tell me about fingerspelling and we ended up angry?"

I nodded.

"You asked me to open my mind. You also suggested I go to your school to talk to Mr. Tate."

"I remember."

"We both went to his office," Dad told me.

"You did?" And the whole time I'd thought they were doing nothing.

"It's one of the best things that's happened since your illness," Mom said. "The doctors never seemed to understand our emotional needs or yours. Mr. Tate really listened to us and answered all our questions. If he couldn't give an answer, he just said so, and in some cases he recommended books for us to read. We love you so much and were so afraid . . . "

Mom's face was filled with emotion. She had puddles in her eyes, too. I leaned over and gave her a kiss. Dad put his hand on mine and said, "We'll talk a lot about it from now on, and we'll work at the day-by-day acceptance you so wisely mentioned in your letter."

I kissed him too.

"I think this is the best birthday I've ever had."

We decided to try out my new closed-caption decoder, so Dad set it up on top of the television set. Once it was working, we found a channel showing a captioned episode of "Cosmos." I was awestruck; I usually felt so left out of shows like that.

Not long after the show was over, Dad said, "Someone's at the back door."

"I'll get it," I told him, thinking it must be Jack coming early.

When I opened the door, though, I found Sara standing on the porch. She looked uncharacteristically unsure of herself, and she was very pale. Although Mrs. Marler had kept us informed on Sara's progress since her accident, no one had seen Sara because she hadn't wanted company.

There was something strange about the way she stood there. Then it hit me. Sara had been hiding. I suddenly noticed that she had a scar on her face. Her beautiful face was marred now. It wasn't that bad a scar, but it must have been devastating for Sara. She had probably taken her beauty for granted in the way I had my hearing.

I sensed how very hard it must have been for her to be standing there, scar showing, pride no doubt bruised, and afraid of the future. My heart went out to her. She'd lost her role as "most beautiful" and "most popular" in one terrible moment.

"I'm glad to see you, Sara," I told her softly. I was going to ask her to come into the kitchen, but when she sat on the steps, I also sat. She was like a doe, and I didn't want to scare her away.

"I wasn't sure you would be," she told me. "I . . . don't know what to say, Gustie." Her eyes drifted from my face down to her feet.

"You don't have to say anything, Sara."

"But I need to, for both of us. I'm so sorry for my selfishness. Somehow my values got all mixed up." She repeated without showing the slightest bit of irritation when I needed her to. "You were right about my need to be 'bestest,' only it took that accident to shake me up enough to see it. It seems like when you got sick, I got worse and turned a lot of my anger loose on you. I'm trying to work it out with a psychologist."

"I'm glad," I told her. "I have lots of faith in you, Sara."

"In me?"

"Don't look so surprised. You are still Sara Marler. Even when I was hurt or felt mad at you, I never gave up hope in you, Sara. I never stopped liking you."

She started to cry then and said through her tears, "You are so forgiving."

Suddenly, I was crying, too, only these tears, unlike some in the past months, were tears of love, not frustration or hurt or anger. I reached out and hugged her and felt her tears as vibrations and little jerks.

When we broke apart, we were both smiling through our tears. Sara said, "There ought to be violins playing."

"Or how about a pipe organ?" I said, and we laughed at ourselves.

She reached for a package a couple of feet away and held it toward me. "I tried to say what I feel in this birthday present. Will you open it out here, though? It's sort of personal."

"Of course." The memory of other birthdays and gifts to and from each other warmed my heart as we sat on the steps. I quickly tore away the polka dotted paper.

It was a unique present. Sara had cut up her old sweatshirt—the one with all the paint smudges symbolizing our shared memories—and used the cloth to cover a large scrapbook, a friendship album. It was full of memories and souvenirs of our years as friends. There was a description of the haunted Henderson house, the apple tree rescue, and many of the other experiences that had marbled our eleven-year friendship. Some pages had quotations by famous people on friendship. There were little poems Sara herself had written, and there were many snapshots that showed us changing over the years. As I turned the pages a little thrill went through me and came out as a smile. "Oh, Sara, this is wonderful."

"Making it helped me to get better," she told me.

Deeply moved, I hugged the album close to my chest. "I love it, Sara," I told her, "and I love you. Thank you for a gift I'll treasure forever."

I asked her to come inside for a piece of birthday cake, but she didn't want to. I thought I understood her reluctance. Coming over had been her first step in showing herself to the outside world again. She needed to take steps in stages that were comfortable and right for her.

Sara was slowly learning to belong again.

When Jack arrived later for birthday cake and our movie date, I was amazed to see a whole crowd of people standing around him.

"Surprise!" they chorused, while Pam and Larry fingerspelled "happy birthday" to me. Lenore and three other girls, a couple of Jack's friends, and to my surprise, Miss Hartman and Mr. Tate rounded out the group of well-wishers.

It was gift enough just to have everyone there, but I also received some wonderful presents. Jack gave me a sterling silver charm in the shape of a hand making the "I love you very much" sign. Pam and Larry brought me a small, beautiful watercolor of a unicorn that I could tell Pam had painted with her skilled hand. Miss Hartman and Mr. Tate gave me a poster that said, "True success is found not in the destination, but in the journey."

It was a very happy evening. Even Mom and Dad seemed to enjoy it. I thought I'd fall off the couch when I saw Larry sign something and Mom and Dad try it clumsily with their hands.

At one point during the evening, I noticed Jasmine sitting on her velvet cushion in the bay window. With her paws tucked under her as she dozed, she looked gorgeous, like some kind of queen.

Then she lazily opened her bright blue eyes. As I watched her, one eye blinked shut. It looked for all the world like a wink. Her mouth seemed to smile, as if to say, "See, Gustie? I'm not the only one you feel close to now."

I winked back.